Karma Chaser

Melanie Miller Hollis

ISBN - 10: 0692896058
ISBN 13: 978-0692896051

To Caleb, Lydia, Natalie, Hope, and Charlie. My tribe. You've opened my mind to theories and concepts I could never have imagined, and I'm eternally grateful for the deep layers that have expanded me as an individual. In your own unique ways, you've taught me that love doesn't give up, that it is something to be fiercely guarded and protected above all else, and that it is ultimately a choice. No matter what, know that I will always choose to love you. Nothing, in fact, can separate you from my love.

Chapter 1

The time for the two prisoners to pass on to the next life drew near. Pacing around the room, her bare feet padded over the worn wooden floors. "You'll never get away with this," one said, but she'd grown accustomed to the chatter and ignored it. Her captives were pathetically weak.

The thought of watching her prisoners die from poisoning simmered like a slow pot of stew in her brain. Poison stew. She'd had weeks to prepare her mind. But when she pictured them foaming at the mouth, gasping for air, she still had to shut the image out of her mind completely. Murder would be hard.

"God, I have such a soft, beautiful heart," she thought to herself, seeing it as her own form of weakness. What was life anyway? If there was really a Creator with a plan, wouldn't their souls just gently pass from this life to the next? And if there wasn't a God, well, then they'd never know the difference anyway. Because they'd be dead.

Reaching for the light switch, she flicked it on and off fifty times. Exactly fifty times. It was a reset of sorts…a way of pushing out the cowardice that haunted her. After the fiftieth click, she took a deep breath. Turning to look at the prisoners, she dared

Page 4 of 198

to picture them dead. If she could see it in her mind, she knew she could follow through.

They were sinners, and Sam had shown her where God wiped out entire groups of people in the Old Testament over sin. "Our killing them will actually gain us favor with the Lord," he'd said. And it had made sense at the time. In scripture, God had used men for His murderous purposes. However, at this point she wasn't completely sure about the validity of God.

"Why does life have to be so complicated?" she wondered, popping up on a table to sit and take in the sight of the captives who were under her complete authority. "If God is real, why would He stay hidden instead of showing His power?"

Bonnie feigned a laugh and finally spoke her thoughts out loud. "I was just wondering…where is your God?" She was addressing her prisoners with a smattering of mockery. "You're getting ready to die, yet He's nowhere to be found. Don't you find that interesting?"

These two, her captives, had faith in God, and she knew it. They'd even called themselves Christians. But what had God done to protect them? Or save them? If He were real and if He were the actual Creator of the universe, couldn't He open the doors of their makeshift prison and set them free? She sneered as she considered the absurdity. The idea of God's protection had turned out to be a joke. The whole idea of God was turning out to be a joke. He protected no one.

The stupid dog had been a pivotal moment for her and had opened her eyes. The little girl with Down syndrome had been out playing in her backyard with her beloved Trudy that day. She was the girl's constant companion and was supposed to be her protector. The curly-haired dog with flopsy ears dutifully followed the girl everywhere. When Trudy spotted Bonnie unlatching the gate, she came running. The dog knew her, so there was no fear, but just in case, Bonnie was prepared with bacon treats. That stupid dog gave up its life for the anticipation of a bacon treat. Such foolishness made Bonnie want to puke.

With a treat in one hand and a serrated hunting knife in the other, she'd cut the dog's throat. In one fail swoop, the dog was as good as dead. As Bonnie thought back on the memory, she mimicked the motion of the knife in her hand as it had slit Trudy's throat. She could still feel the unexpected rush. Miss Charity, the little girl with the extra chromosome, had witnessed her beloved dog bleeding out with big, round eyes and a mind that was unable to comprehend what had happened.

Bonnie had watched Miss Charity lay on the ground and place her head upon the dog's head. She closed the gate behind her, and when the gate clicked shut, the little girl had raised up to watch her leave. The dog's blood was crimson red on Miss Charity's cheek. She then laid her head back down. Bonnie imagined that she'd remain there with her companion until her mother found them both.

For a split second, she'd felt some remorse. Miss Charity, after all, was the best one of the whole Montgomery bunch…Philip included. It has been required of Bonnie though. Sam had told her, "If you can slit that dog's throat and deal with the fact that you took its life, knowing how much that dog means to a special-needs kid, you'll be more prepared to take the life of a human." It had been part of her training. God hadn't protected that dog or the little girl because He was either not real or unconnected. Bonnie could've just as easily slit both of their throats that day. At least that's what she told Sam, but deep in her heart, she was thankful beyond words that he hadn't expected it of her.

The dog was innocent, but her current prisoners weren't. "The wages of sin is death," Sam had told her. "It's not your fault the dog had to die; it's the prisoners' fault. They made you do it. Remember that."

And she did.

"This is all your fault," she said. "All of it is." She felt the heat of anger rise up into her cheeks. "Your death will be because of your sin." Bonnie bit her words off, considering how she would be a part of their death.

Since the day she'd killed Trudy, she'd been required to take the life of six other animals, both cats and dogs. "Seven," Sam had said, "is God's perfect and most holy number." He'd explained how God would see her act as a humble sacrifice, holy and acceptable in His sight, if she took the time to kill exactly seven. She'd done it for Sam and for the idea of God, but mostly for Mary.

All those deaths were on the heads of her prisoners. They had transgressed against the ancient laws of scripture. In the Old Testament, animals were killed for the atonement of sin. It was God's way. It was now Bonnie's way. Mary had to die.

Chapter 2

It all began when the local gossip sites started touting the wedding as the most ostentatious the city had ever witnessed. It was true, of course. The happy couple had spared no expense, even though they'd decided to get married on the spur of the moment. This was not a first marriage for either, and being in the news was something they'd become accustomed to. The bride, especially, lived for the attention.

Viv's services had been requested for the wedding planning and decor. She wanted to decline, but her family needed the money. Even though her true vocation was working with children who are differently abled during the week, her weekends were now booking up with weddings. As with any true talent, it didn't take long for her to get noticed and for word to spread.

It was late spring, and the day was unusually mild. The weather couldn't have been more perfect for an outdoor countryside wedding. The bride had rented out the Coffey Barn, a quaint venue on several rolling acres tucked between the hills of the Tennessee Valley. Surrounded by gentle peaks of pine that were clearly visible in the distance, the setting offered a rustic wooden barn with soaring ceilings, a cozy covered side porch, and a sprawling outside pergola.

The grand, expansive pergola, draped in sparkling globe string lights and airy organza, would be where the bride and groom would vow eternal love to one another. White wooden folding chairs stood in perfect lines beneath the wooden frame as though they were soldiers awaiting orders from their new queen. And a center aisle was carefully lined with white rose petals, set to welcome the one-of-a-kind designer wedding gown with plunging neckline and layered organza skirt. Every detail had been executed with the greatest of attention.

Following the ceremony, five trendy food trucks would pull up on the property to offer a plethora of freshly prepared eclectic dining choices including Thai, French, Mexican, Italian, and southern fare. It would be an endless banquet of richly inspired food from all over the world, topped off by a traditional four-tiered wedding cake, modeled after the bride's designer gown, and a fully stocked ice cream bar. All guests would sit around round-top tables inside the barn to dine.

To top it all, a live band would be set up on the out-door porch, welcoming the guests to dance beneath the stars. Pillared candles placed in large lanterns would add to the natural ambience. The wedding would begin at 4:00 p.m., but there was no end time. Who, after all, would dare place a time limit on the celebration of true love?

White roses and tulips were the flowers of choice and seemed to explode about the space, making it a virtual garden event. Per the bride's instructions, hundreds of the flowers had been carefully tucked within custom-made rustic boxes and were hanging upside down from the ceiling of the barn, festooning the space with bursts of white. Those same rustic boxes could be found all over the grounds, along with glass containers of varying shapes and sizes, filled with the classic simplicity of white roses and tulips. The flowers hung from tree branches, dangled from fence posts, and sat proudly as the centerpieces of tables, boasting the impending union.

Viv couldn't help herself. As she approached the groom, her ex-brother-in-law, one last time before he was a married man once again, she held out her hand, offering a roll of sour candy. "SweeTarts for your sweetheart?" she asked, eyebrows raised.

Taking the candy from her hand, he rolled it around in his fingers for a few seconds, remembering all the times he'd said those words to his first love. She'd been his first date, his first dance, his first kiss, and his first wife. She was the mother of his children, the one who could make him laugh when he felt like crying, and the only one allowed to call him Chief. Why had things gone so terribly wrong?

He and Mary had pulled even closer together when Miss Charity was born with Down syndrome and had managed to weather the many medical procedures she'd had on her heart since birth. It was when Wills, their oldest, had become addicted to a party lifestyle that included heavy alcohol and marijuana use that they began to grow apart. But when Wills rejected Mary, preferring estrangement over relationship, the best part of her had died. Philip was certain she'd never been the same.

Philip's affair with Bonnie hadn't helped matters, of course, but what was he to do? His wife had gone into a funk at the time, barely having any time at all for him. And the blond bombshell was throwing herself at him constantly. There was a risk-taking irreverence about Bonnie that made her much more than seductive. The woman was a full-blown temptress who relentlessly pursued him, refusing to give up. Eventually Philip had caved, even though the affair itself was short lived. But Mary had been in the direct path of the destruction. Wills had not been the only one to break her heart.

And the fiasco with the cult? It had cost them their home and had nearly taken down their business. Mary had wanted to believe everything the cult leaders had told her. If she'd follow all their rules, clinging tightly to the Mosaic Law in scripture, the cult leaders told her Miss Charity's heart would be healed. As any vulnerable mother might be tempted to do, she followed the rules and regulations to a *T*. She'd even taken Philip back as her husband since the religious sect forbade separation and divorce. But in the end, the cult was a farce, and all added together, the emotional toll was too much. Miss Charity, her youngest child, still had an aneurysm in her heart and had remained nonverbal. It was amazing to consider the toll one extra chromosome could take on one so young. Though Mary had sought God in humility and faith, He'd proven to be nothing more than the lead role of an epic fairytale. Miracles were counterfeit superpowers that didn't exist.

"Mary told me to move on," he replied, frowning at Viv, "so I'm moving on."

Tossing the SweeTarts toward Viv, she snagged them from the air. "Who are you trying to kid? You'll never move on, Philip," she said, aggravation spelled prominently across her face.

He knew what she said was true.

Chapter 3

GiGi and Poppy, Mary's parents, had taken Miss Charity and her big sister, Tate, to the wedding. Mary, all alone in the old white house she used to share with Philip, opted not to go. Even though she knew the storyline, she lived each and every day as a cruel death dream of sorts, the stabbing pain in her heart very real. Chief was marrying Bonnie.

Wills, acutely aware that his father was to wed Bonnie Cutless, assumed his mom would be taking his younger siblings to the wedding since she rarely let Miss Charity out of her sight. Needing money for his living expenses, and expecting the house to be empty, he took the opportunity to pay a visit to his old homeplace. Climbing up the front stairs, he reached under the door mat and retrieved a hidden key.

"As dependable as mice and cheese." He chuckled, unlocking the door.

Mary was busy sweeping the kitchen floor when he bounded into the room. "Wills," she gasped, not believing the sight before her. He stood more than six feet tall, but all Mary could see was her little boy. He'd come home. "I'm so glad you're here," she said as tears sprang from her eyes and trailed down her cheeks. "I've been in this annoying death dream for such a long time, and I've wondered why you haven't shown up." Laying the broom against the countertop, she made her way to give him a hug.

"Death dream?" he asked, stepping back from his mother with a look of disgust. "What in the hell are you talking about?" His dad had mentioned that Mary was having a mental battle with anxiety, but he'd never mentioned that she'd lost her mind. "Listen, I just came to get a few things from my room and then I'll be outta here, all right?"

Leaping up the staircase two steps at a time, Wills was out of her sight within seconds. Mary stood with a blank stare on her face. She was confused. She'd been fighting to stay in the death dream long enough to see her son, yet now that he'd shown up, nothing was as she hoped it would be. Wearing a worn, fuzzy, gray sweatshirt and a cut-off pair of denim shorts, Mary braced herself by holding onto the kitchen counter. A pony-tail hung down and kissed her neck. From behind, she looked very much to be the age of one of her son's peers, but stress was wearing on her. Face to face, the lines of worry were showing.

Mary considered picking up her broom and continuing to clean, ignoring the death dream altogether. "Why entertain such madness?" she asked herself. All the while wondering what Wills was doing upstairs. Why had he come by?

She finally made the decision to go to him, to say good-bye and to tell him she loved him. Maybe this was a test, and perhaps dealing with Wills would allow her to go to the next step of purgatory. Yes, facing her son head on was the answer. Pushing herself away from the counter, Mary shoved her fears away and forged up the staircase.

As she climbed, Mary recalled how she'd finally determined that she died during Miss Charity's birth. For many years, she thought she was living in reality, but when life had gone so haywire, she put the pieces together. She was actually in some type of holding pattern where her spirit hung between heaven and earth. Before reaching eternal heaven, there was obviously a lesson or two more for her to learn, and it was up to her to figure it all out. She needed to explain it all to Wills. To help him understand.

"Wills?" she asked, knocking on his bedroom door.

He didn't answer.

"Wills?" she asked again, this time pushing the door open. But he was nowhere to be found. Trophies and ribbons lined his walls, displaying the many years he'd played sports. Breathing in through her nose, she could still smell his scent. A hint of cologne, a laundry basket still filled with dirty socks, and Doritos chips. How many times had she sat in the floor of her son's room, longing to be near him again?

Making her way down the hallway, she heard some clunking noises in her parents' bedroom. "Wills, are you in there?" she asked, opening their door.

"No, I'm not really in here, and I'm not really Wills… this is a death dream, you crazy lady." He insulted her, continuing to root through the bureau belonging to his grandparents. Finding some cash, he shoved it deep down in his pocket. Seeing his mother standing in the doorway caused him to want to be physically sick. Nausea swept over him like a thick looming fog. He had to get out of there before he suffocated from the pain.

"Tell GiGi and Pops I'll make sure I pay them back someday since they've shown me such love and devotion." Sarcasm oozed from every word as he spoke. The family had all agreed that if he wanted to live by his own rules, he'd need to live on his own, supporting himself. Wills felt like he'd been dumped, like the people who'd once believed in him most had turned their backs on him. Part of him wanted his mother to rush to him, to hold him tight, and to save him. He was in way deeper than she could imagine. But another part of him wanted her to feel the same hurt he was feeling.

"Go ahead and make fun of my death dream, but you're the main reason I know I'm dead…and I wish you'd listen and let me explain," she said, pleading with him as tears soaked her face. "None of this is real. It can't be real. All of this brokenness cannot be our lives." Her head shook with every word, displaying the body language of a woman laden with denial.

Wills, still standing near the bureau, pointed his finger toward the ground with intense furor. "This is real!" he shouted, veins popping out from his temples. "God Almighty, why can't I have a normal mom?"

Mary felt her knees nearly give away beneath her. There she was, in a debate with the death dream version of her son, trying to figure out what purpose seeing her son stealing from her parents served from an eternal perspective. In the real world, was he struggling? Did he need her prayers? What was the message? It all felt so real.

"Listen, there are things that I know," she began, hoping to resolve the conflict that rippled beneath her skin and trickled up in the form of a bitter cold chill. "I know my Wills would never reject me or turn to alcohol and drugs to solve his problems… and he'd rather starve or be homeless than to steal from anyone, especially from his family." She spoke the words out loud, so she'd believe them. If Mary knew anything, she knew her son.

Trudy, the family's dog, stood with her head raised high by Mary's side. She'd always favored Wills but instinctively felt a need to stand with Mary.

"You actually think you're dead, don't you?" he asked, speaking down to her as if she were nothing. "Yet *you* judge *me*? God, how did I ever get mixed up in a family like this?" Walking toward her, he expected her to move from the doorway to let him slide by. She didn't.

"I'd love to stay and chat with you, Mother, but I've got somewhere to be," he said, standing toe to toe with her. "Move out of my way, or I'll push you out of my way."

Mary's heart raced and her hands shook. It was a panic attack. "I'm just trying to figure out why you're like this in my death dream because it seems to me that you'd love me. Even in my afterlife. Because I've always loved you, Wills." Mary's voice shook as she spoke, but she worked to overcome the ensuing rise of alarm that was taking over her body.

Wills laughed. "You call kicking me out of my home love? How dare you even say that you love me! You're a fake, Mary Montgomery. I've seen the *real* you, and not only do I not love you, I don't even like you!"

His words were sharp. Even in her state of purgatory, they stung. The inflection in his voice reflected what was in his heart, and it didn't feel like a dream. He appeared to be intentional with every word.

Mary had forced Wills to leave out of love, and that was while she was in the death dream. It had been one of many purgatory tests. What kind of parent would financially support a lifestyle that would eventually kill her child both spiritually and physically? Surely that was a test she'd passed. But maybe not.

"None of this is really happening," she whispered as she made an effort to take a deep, cleansing breath. The tightness in her chest wouldn't allow it. Grasping her heart, she tried again to take a deep breath without success. "Mary," she murmured, speaking out loud to herself, "hold onto the fact that in reality, Wills still loves you very much...and right now, out in the real world, he is missing you. Because you're dead." Yes, this was part of her death dream. The deep breath came.

Wills stood before her with horror and disbelief in his eyes. Mary, in response, felt worthless. The last thing she ever wanted was to be an embarrassment to her kids.

Looking up at the one she'd held in her arms as a baby before he crawled or took his first steps, she addressed him with compassion and honesty. "I think I'm getting ready to awaken from this part of my death dream, Wills, so I just wanted to say good-bye to you and to tell you that I'm proud of you and I love you so much. We will see each other again someday when you reach heaven, honey. I'm sure of it." Mary sighed a breath of relief. Her pulse slowed down to a normal pace. She'd said what she wanted to say and was feeling sure this was a check off her purgatory list.

"Wow, this is sad," Wills finally replied, his voice calm and cold. "Dad mentioned that you were a bit off kilter, but he didn't tell me you were ready for a rubber room and a straight-jacket."

What was he saying? Philip had told their son she was crazy?

"This isn't real…" Mary said, her heart rate beginning to pick up steam again, "none of this is real." Fighting to stand her ground, she continued. "Satan, do you hear me? I'm onto your twisted game, and this isn't real no matter how hard you work to confuse me!" she screamed, her eyes darting around the room as she carried on a one-sided conversation with thin air. "You've been allowed to test me, but you will not win! My son loves me and I know I'm not crazy!"

As Mary melted, Wills's bewilderment festered into disgust. "I don't know what kind of sick game you're playing, Mom, but I can assure you that you aren't dead and this isn't a death dream. You actually kicked me out of my home, and on that day, my love for you ended. Here me say this, Mother," he said, his tone flat and filled with hate. "I will never love you again."

Pushing his mother aside with a rough shove of his shoulder, Wills barged through the door and bolted down the stairs. Mary, entering full panic mode, ran after him.

"Wills, please stop!" she yelled, trying to catch up with him. "This is a death dream; do you hear me? None of this is real! It can't be! I know you love me!"

On the last few steps, Mary tripped and fell. "Wills!" she shouted, but he was gone. Piercing pain shot through her ankle and up through her leg. Pulling her phone from her back pocket, she dialed her mother.

Chapter 4

Wills's life was spiraling out of control, and he knew it. After being caught by the police with marijuana, he'd been placed on probation. His dad's parents had paid a hefty fee to accomplish that much. Without them, he could've faced some jail time. Because he was unwilling to give up the name of his supplier, however, the offense went on his record.

His family had been aware of his heavy alcohol use, but the marijuana charge came as a complete surprise. What none of them knew was that he was also addicted to Adderall, a "study drug" that he'd been introduced to by some friends at school. Wills had become, for all intents and purposes, a junkie.

His addiction had begun innocently enough. He'd been booted out of his parent's home after he fell into heavy partying that led to several speeding tickets, failing grades, and a bad attitude. Although he acted like he was repulsed by their rejection of him, the truth was that he understood why they did what they did. He knew they would never condone his rebellion. The rules had been laid out for him, and he'd broken them all, plain and simple.

The heavy partying left Wills tired, which made studying and retaining knowledge nearly impossible, so when someone offered him a pill that would help solve his problem, he took it. The Adderall was a miracle drug. The first pill was given to him as a gift, and it had boosted his energy so much that he was able to stay up all night to cram for an exam. At that point, he was hooked. It happened that fast.

Wills's family was a disaster. During most of his lifetime, his family had provided a solid foundation he could count on. Whenever he had challenges with school, sports, or friends, he could always feel his feet planted firmly on the ground of home. But when his dad had an affair and then moved out, everything changed. Wills was lost.

As he ran across the front lawn of the Ocoee home, he replayed the sound of his mother screaming out his name, trying to convince him that her life had become a dream. Her life was so difficult, she had to conjure up a death dream to deal with it. How had life flipped upside down?

A friend was parked on the road, waiting for him. Wills pulled open the passenger door and hopped in. "Let's go," he said, glancing back over his right shoulder at the old white house when they pulled away. Leaving in that car felt like leaving his troubles behind. Away from home Wills could be a different person. That's how he survived.

On the drive back to Chattanooga though, he felt the familiar pang of longing that he'd felt so many times before. More than anything else in the world, he wished to travel back in time to the days when he galloped through the house with Miss Charity on his shoulders, pretending to be her favorite pony… to the nights when he'd stay up late watching reruns of *I Love Lucy* with Tate, his other sister, giggling until their sides hurt as they ate microwave popcorn. And his momma, she'd never know how much he longed to sit and talk to her, to feel her ruffle his hair with her fingertips, and to tell her everything that was locked up in his heart. But he couldn't. She'd be so disappointed if she knew the secrets he was hiding.

Pulling a wad of tissue from his pocket, Wills found a few orange pills. Without any water to wash them down, he popped two in his mouth and swallowed hard. Within a few minutes, he'd feel much better.

Chapter 5

"All righty, Philip, I've kept my big mouth shut long enough, hoping against hope that you'd come to your gall-darned senses." GiGi barged in and was fit to be tied. During times of great distress, her southern twang shown a bit more brash than usual. "But here we are on your wedding day, aren't we? And you're set to marry Bonnie Cutless." GiGi still couldn't believe it. "Good Lord, am I being pranked? Is this one of those practical joke reality TV shows?"

She gadded about the the room, acting as if she was looking for hidden cameras, but she knew full well this was all very real. Philip just stood by and let her do what she did best. As usual, drama was GiGi's tool of choice. After making her point, she turned to stare down her former son-in-law.

"I want to puke, Philip, right here and now on my expensive dress. Does that make you happy?" Lifting an open hand up to her mouth, GiGi pretended to gag obnoxiously. "Is there an alternate reality where this union actually makes sense? If so, I want to go there, unpack my glad rags, and sit a spell for laughs…because it must be a crazy place where anything is possible!"

GiGi had stormed into the room where the groom was getting dressed and was stomping around like a bull preparing to charge. She hadn't taken the time to realize that Philip was half naked. It wouldn't have mattered though, if she had noticed. The woman was going to continue preaching until God Himself came into the room to save Philip from the sinful clutch of the Jezebel woman, Bonnie Cutless.

"Perhaps in that alternate reality," she said, continuing, "where even Bonnie Cutless can become a respectable woman, old Pops could morph into the likes of George Clooney…if so, I think I could dig that." She laughed, poking fun. Finding humor in the current situation was necessary for her sanity. She knew that, and so did Philip.

Philip's father, Pip, was in the room as well. GiGi had come in like such a sudden gust of wind, he hadn't thought about the inappropriateness of it all. His son was standing in nothing more than his T-shirt and boxer shorts. Standing quickly to his feet, he reprimanded her on behalf of his son. "This is highly inappropriate…you really shouldn't be in here. Please leave."

"Wouldn't you know it? Just when I was beginning to find a speck of happiness in this hideous day… you know, daydreaming about my hubby transforming into the likes of George Clooney in your son's self-made alternate reality"—she huffed, rolling her eyes—"old haughty pants, akin to the likes of President Donald Trump, had to show up, pipe up, and zap me plum out of it." GiGi had dated Pip a lifetime ago; in fact, she'd dumped him. As a result, he presented no hindrance for her. In her mind, she'd always have the upper hand when it came to Pip.

"Are you calling *me* Donald Trump?" he asked, clearly insulted. Sucking in his stomach, patting down his hair, and standing as straight as his back would allow, he changed his tenor to a softer tone and added, "I'm nothing like him, and you know it."

"All I can say, boss hog, is if the shoe fits, you gotta wear it," she crooned, sticking her nose up in the air in the snootiest of ways. "And by the way, I've already seen that bubble belly of yours, so just exhale and blow it back up."

Pip was aghast. "Bubble belly?" he asked, not believing her nerve.

"Bubble belly and a big mouth, which is not a good combination…but if you'd lay off carbs and cobbler, it would cure *one* of your problems really quick. Are you still drinking sweet tea like it's your primary life source?"

Sweet tea had always been his favorite beverage, even during the days when the two had dated. Pip, not knowing quite how to handle the barbs, took a seat. "Yes, I do still drink sweet tea," he answered, folding his arms. "But I only have cobbler once a week…twice a week at most."

"With ice cream?" she sang, needling him further.

If he wasn't such a gentleman, Pip might've stood again and slapped her silly. What business was it of hers? He was far from overweight, but *had* put on a few extra pounds since moving back to Tennessee. The popular meat and three restaurants that pop up on every corner in the south, offering a feast of fresh baked rolls, buttermilk fried chicken, and homemade cobblers, had been a bigger temptation than he'd expected.

Darn the woman for reading him so well. "Yes, of course I eat my cobbler with ice cream," he answered. Why was he answering her? Lord, she drove him crazy.

"Well I'd say that explains it," she crowed, feeling full of herself and acting as sassy as ever. "I could help you with an exercise regimen if you're interested, because I'm like the Good Samaritan of the Bible who helps those in need…but right now, I've got some business to take care of with your half-baked son, and I'm gonna say what I've come to say whether you like it or not."

Pip wasn't going to dare say another word. His eyes flashed toward his son. It was now Philip's turn to get an earful. Pip took a deep breath. He was off the hook.

Realizing his former mother-in-law was on another one of her rolls, Philip knew trying to stop her would be equal to halting a hurricane…not only impossible, but a complete waste of energy. Whatever she'd come into the room to say would be said whether he liked it or not.

Battening down the hatches and bracing himself for the storm to come, he sighed. "I'm listening, but make it quick since I *am* on a tight schedule today." He quickly yanked on his tuxedo pants and walked over to grab hold of the back of the chair where his dad was seated to steady himself. Nodding in the affirmative, he gave her permission to begin her full diatribe.

GiGi could've pinched his head off. The longer she was in the room with Philip, the redder her cheeks became. "You made vows for better or for worse when you married my daughter. It was a contract with the Almighty, in case you've forgotten." Her finger was wagging as she spoke. "And I know you still love her, which means you're just after sex, sex, and more sex with that slut you're about to marry. You're a horny toad, Philip—excuse my brashness—but that ain't no reason to marry somebody. She's Delilah and you're Sampson, except she won't be buzzing off your hair. Mark my words, that woman will cut your balls off and hang 'em from her car mirror if you don't let her rule over your life from this day forward."

She was over the top, yet it was her authentic self.

"She really is a nut job," Pip mumbled, bending over to place his head in his hands. "No pun intended, of course."

His comment was not taken lightly by the old bird. "You better wake up, Pip, because your son is getting ready to make a monumental mistake. He's fallen into the abyss with a she-devil who's ready and able to take his manhood," GiGi answered, pacing around the room in her high heels. "I'm just a messenger from God. I've been praying and fasting for God to give Philip a clear sign that this marriage didn't need to happen, and I just got off the phone with Mary. She's been in an accident at home. Wills came by and they got into a fight and..."

Philip perked up with sudden panic. "Wills and Mary? Is everything OK?"

"No, you big dummy, things are *not* OK," she said, addressing her former son-in-law plainly. "What did you not hear about me saying there has been a fight and that Mary has been in an accident? She's laying at the foot of her stairs, dying for all I know, while you stand here in those tuxedo pants, acting like a fool. Your family is broken, Philip, but that don't mean you have a right to throw it away and marry somebody else—"

Before she could finish her thought, Philip grabbed his keys and ran out the door. The wedding had come to a screeching halt.

Chapter 6

Bonnie, alone in the bridal room, was stunned to hear the news. Philip had left her behind to be Mary's savior. Enrobed in her magnificent wedding gown, prepared to walk down the aisle to become Philip's queen, she gazed upon herself in the full-length mirror. "Mary, Mary, quite contrary, you've triumphed once again," she said, tracing the reflection of her face with the tip of her finger, "but taking my man on my wedding day is an unpardonable sin."

Anger coursed through her veins like white-water rapids on a stormy day. She'd worked to win the heart of Philip, and every step of her plan had been implemented to the letter. She'd even gone to counseling and had been religiously taking meds for what the psychiatrist had labeled a mental disorder. Was she the one with the disorder? Wasn't it Mary who was staging some sort of emergency in order to steal Philip away from her?

Bonnie looked at her image in the mirror. Her body was in perfect shape. Mary was ordinary and plain when compared to her, so why couldn't Philip let her go? What was so special about Mary?

She smacked the mirror hard with the palm of her hand and almost allowed herself to cry, but a tap on the door caused her to quickly regain composure.

***

When Philip arrived at the old house on Ocoee Street, he didn't even stop to consider that it was no longer his home. Forgetting all proper etiquette, he jammed his car into park, and without turning off the ignition, tore like a banshee into the house.

"Mary!" he yelled, as he threw the door open. Not knowing what had happened between his former wife and son, he couldn't help but fear the worst. Wills was no longer the son they'd once known. Vengeance and rage had taken hold of a heart that was once full of love and kindness. It was Philip's fault; he hadn't been the leader of the family the way he should've been. The weight of it all nearly caused him to hyperventilate. "Mary, where are you?"

Mary couldn't believe her ears. It was Philip's voice. "Chief, I'm in here on the floor," she answered, her heart settling down, knowing the man who'd always been there for her had arrived. He'd been a part of her life since she was a teenager and had always made her feel safe and secure. They were divorced now, but those old feelings still remained intact.

After careful inspection, Philip determined Mary had either a very badly sprained or broken ankle. Scooping her up into his arms, he carried her out to his car and gently placed her inside. The hospital was only a short drive away. Her knight in shining armor had everything under control.

***

Bonnie, relieved that anyone had thought to check on her, immediately made her way to the door and swung it wide open.

"Well, hey there, darlin', could I steal a few minutes of your time?" The man standing before her had a scruffy beard, unkempt hair, piercing eyes, and a thin, athletic build. He wasn't the most handsome man, but he was rugged in a very L. L. Bean sort of way…worn Levi's, Justin work boots, and a khaki colored Field Blazer.

Bonnie, leaning against the open door, offered a slight grin. "Why not, Sam? Come on in." As he entered, she closed the door behind him and locked it. Whatever Viv's husband had to say would be more exciting than spending time alone in the bridal chamber.

Skipping small talk, Sam didn't even mention the fact that Bonnie had been dumped on her wedding day. Instead, after taking a seat and placing his right foot upon his left knee, he made a statement. "I've heard an awful lot of stories about you, Bonnie, and I think we may have some key things in common."

Intrigued, Bonnie answered, "Tell me all about those key things, Sam. It just so happens that my schedule is completely free today."

Chapter 7

Philip's parents, Mary's parents, Viv, and all the kids promptly left the wedding venue and made their way to Ocoee Street to await news from Mary and Philip.

"I really liked Bonnie," said Aggie, as she meandered to the sofa, trying to make the most of an awkward situation. Philip's swift exit from the wedding had left them all feeling rattled. "I guess she won't forgive Philip for this though."

Because Aggie and GiGi had never gotten along in their lives, Aggie was happy that her son was finally making a break from Mary. And Bonnie, in full Bonnie fashion, had gone overboard to prove herself worthy of Aggie's son. She had two primary things going for her. First, she slathered so much sugar on her would-be mother-in-law that it sickened everyone who knew better. And second, she hated GiGi just as much as Aggie hated her.

GiGi couldn't be silent. "Would you please get your head out of your butt, Aggie? I mean it. Wake the hell up!" Whenever GiGi felt especially emotional, she was known to fling a cuss word or two. "Bonnie Cutless is as crazy as a loon and has been buttering up to you so she could steal Philip from Mary."

GiGi was wasting her breath. It was no use. Aggie, unwilling to see the truth, was blinded by the compliments and gifts Bonnie always gave her. "You just can't stand that your perfect daughter has been dumped by my son," she retorted, snapping a bit too hard.

For the sake of the grandchildren, GiGi tried to be civil to Pip and Aggie, though she detested their pompous, know-it-all attitudes. After Pip's retirement, they'd waltzed back into town and had tried to take over GiGi's church. GiGi had always valued being known as the most faith-filled woman of all the members. But now Pip was pushing Aggie to be more popular in the church than GiGi, and Aggie was pursuing the challenge with a vengeance. If the truth be told, GiGi was feeling the pressure. And now, that same woman was in her house taking a cut at her daughter.

"The Good Book says to love your neighbor, and so I invited you over here today to wait on your son since he's with Mary and that's the hospitable thing to do…but after five minutes, you've already insulted me and worn out your welcome." Turning to Pip, she said, "You better get your wife outta my house before I clobber her."

The house was now officially owned by Mary's parents. GiGi and Poppy had sold their own home to buy it when Philip and Mary had found themselves in unexpected financial despair. If that house could tell stories, oh, the stories it would tell. For many years, it had been filled with joy as Mary and Philip lived out their romance. No journey is complete, however, without both mountains and valleys. Their mountains had been steep, complete with jagged edges and harrowing cliffs. And the valleys? They'd been more like caves, cutting into the dark, putrid core of the earth.

Instead of shoring up their gear, pulling together, and taking on the excruciating path with hands interlocked tightly together, Philip and Mary had allowed the terrain to pull them apart. The house now stood as a beacon, displaying their failures and brokenness. It was poetic, then, that on the day of Bonnie and Philip's wedding, an accident in that old white house would pull them together once more.

Hours after admittance into the emergency room, it was determined that Mary's ankle was broken. Thankfully it was a clean break that likely would not require surgery, but she'd be in a medical boot for at least eight weeks.

In all the tither, Mary hadn't even thought to ask Philip about his wedding. On the way home, she finally broached the subject. "So, Chief, where's Bonnie?"

*****

The conversation with Sam was interesting, to say the least. Bonnie was at her wits end, and Sam knew it. Any woman jilted by a man whose allegiance is to another is ripe for an act of retaliation, but Bonnie Cutless wasn't an ordinary woman by a long shot. Sam knew she was ready for the dose of information he had to feed her. He'd come with a plan.

"How do I know I can trust you?" she asked, measuring the man who'd promised to help her take down Mary as long as she'd help him take down Viv.

Sam snickered as he recalled first meeting his in-laws. At that time, they'd seemed genuine with their interest in following God's true ways. Now, though, they referred to his church as a cult. In the Old Testament, God authorized men to slay entire towns and classes of people who were opposed to His ways. He was now authorizing Sam to get rid of his wife…her sister, Mary, would be collateral damage.

"It's pretty plain and simple…you don't know if you can trust me or not," he replied arrogantly, grinning, "but I don't know if I can trust you either, Bonnie, so we're in the same boat."

Instead of giving a curt response, which would've been a typical move on her part, Bonnie stood staring at the man who'd offered her the thing she wanted most in life at that moment. In response, he stood and held out his hand for her to shake. Should she make a deal with the devil?

It was too good to pass up. She'd been jilted on her wedding day and was now nothing more than a laughing stock. Stepping toward him, Bonnie took his hand in hers, but in a calculated move, pulled him in close to her and gave him a soft kiss on his cheek. "Yes, I think I want to make that deal," she whispered in his ear before softly biting his earlobe. If this was going to be a team effort, she needed to have the upper hand.

Sam remained stoic, trying his level best to not allow Bonnie to see the impact her unexpected move had on him. She didn't need to see anything though. Bonnie had been wrapping men around her finger for as far back as she could remember. "Now get out of here," she added, playfully pushing him away toward the door and giving him a soft pat on his rear end. "This former bride needs to slip out of her wedding gown and move on to bigger and better things."

Closing the door behind him, Sam paused briefly and then turned to reopen it. Bonnie had already pulled her straps down around her waist, so at the sight of Sam, she quickly covered her bare breasts with her arms. Sam thought his knees would buckle at the sight, but he didn't let on. "Just wanted to ask one more thing before I go," he said, his voice shaking from the sight of the gorgeous blonde. Her full breasts were barely covered by her slender arms, and his imagination immediately went into overdrive.

Bonnie noticed.

"Sure, Sam," she replied, her voice intentionally seductive, "ask away." This was too easy. She already had Sam in the palm of her hand.

"Yeah, um, I was just wondering if you were the one behind Philip's famous penis pic?" Even as he asked the question, he felt childish for asking it. Here he was standing in front of the most beautiful woman he'd ever seen, and she was barely clothed, yet he was asking about another man's penis.

Bonnie allowed her arms to move just enough so that Sam could get a better view of her breasts, but pretended it was an unconscious move on her part. He was such a fool. "Sam," she replied, "you need to go ahead and get out of here so I can get out of this dress, OK, hon?"

He retreated quickly, mumbling something about being sorry for asking such a stupid question. When he was out of the room, Bonnie shook her head and allowed her dress to fall to her feet. Why were men such easy prey?

As Sam pulled away in his car, he thought about the question he'd asked Bonnie. If she'd been responsible for Philip's penis photo, which had made its way all over town, she was more of a mastermind than he'd anticipated. That photo was probably the final nail in the coffin for Philip and Mary.

Regardless, Bonnie was a vixen, and he'd have to keep his wits about him when in her presence or he might fall into sin. A part of him wanted to fall into sin with her…to fall into bed with her. She'd kissed him and nibbled at his ear, hadn't she? Sam felt his confidence soar.

Rolling down his window, the bearded man took in the sight that represented all the planning and hard work his wife had put into the day to make it a perfect wedding for Philip and Bonnie. Compared to Bonnie, Viv was old-fashioned and frumpy. He'd made every effort to have a holy marriage, but she'd ruined it when she began questioning their church and its doctrine. Who was she to question her husband's beliefs? If he wanted her to wear skirts down to her ankles, to wear blouses that covered her chest and shoulders, and to wear a small feminine head covering, she should be eager to please. After all, at her age, Viv was lucky to get a husband.

There was also Michael, Viv's old flame, of course. Sam had taken care of him, and even though Viv had sworn she didn't have an affair with Michael, he

wasn't sure. Viv had to be dealt with. The sacred-
ness of his religion depended on it. This was about
defending God's righteousness.

It had been years since Sam had listened to any
music other than messianic music, but as he pulled
out of the Coffey Barn parking area, he switched his
radio to a classic rock station. Immediately recognizing the song, he turned it up even louder and
sang along. The partnership with Bonnie would be
an interesting one. God, in his infinite wisdom, had
brought along a magnificent woman to help him
take down his wife. "God is good," he thought,
speeding away.

Chapter 8

Rose and Ruby would never be bounced around by the foster care system again; their official adoption was set to be finalized within days. Because of early childhood trauma, both battled Reactive Attachment Disorder (RAD) and Oppositional Defiant Disorder (ODD), which made parenting them a challenging job. But Sam, only concerned about appearances, had insisted they adopt the girls in spite of the behavior challenges.

"You're probably barren since you're not pregnant yet, and if we want to honor God through our lives, we have to become a family," he'd fussed one night after yet another pregnancy test came back negative. "God made man and woman to populate the earth and to spread His ways. That's the whole reason we were created."

Sam's religious views were contrary to how Viv had been raised. Sam saw God as an angry father who sought to control and punish His children; Viv had been taught that He was a loving father who gravitated toward forgiveness, love, grace, and mercy. She'd explained how it sometimes takes time to get pregnant, and with her being in her forties, that it might take longer. She expressed her willingness to explore fertility options, but he wouldn't hear of it. It was the natural way or adoption.

"Trust me, if you were living in God's will, you'd be plenty fertile. That's how I know you're living in sin. Whether you've physically cheated with Michael or just thought about it in your depraved mind, you're being punished." His accusatory words stung. "And you've also gone and questioned my beliefs, which means you're questioning God's word," he continued. "So the Father has removed the blessing of motherhood from you, Viv. It's as clear as that pathetic pout on your face. And I'm being punished for your sins as well. You've whored yourself…and you've questioned God's ways. This is all on you."

She'd sworn to him that she'd never cheated with her old boyfriend. It was a lie, but she didn't care. This was about survival. Sam didn't believe her and had hit her time and time again with a wooden paddle. She'd lost count of how many times she'd been disciplined by her husband. The tool he used had been handmade by a member of the church to use on Rose and Ruby, but he'd used it on her. Viv had been thrown over his lap where he'd bruised her legs, buttocks, and back. The longer she stayed with him, the more frequently he beat her. And the abuse was becoming more severe.

How had she gotten into this mess? And why did she allow it to continue? The shame of not being able to bear a child weighed on her. She did feel like a failure. If a woman can't conceive, what good is she? She felt like a disgrace. Viv was losing herself.

*****

"Rose," GiGi asked as they waited on Mary and Philip to return home from the hospital, "is everything all right in your home, love bug?" The two were busy changing sheets and fluffing pillows, getting Mary's bed ready for her to come home.

Now seven years old, Rose had grown to love GiGi as much as was possible for a young girl who'd suffered so much neglect in her short lifetime. GiGi didn't pull punches. If something was on the woman's mind, there was no filter. And something was definitely on her mind.

"Yeah, everything's fine," she answered, diligently pulling the fitted sheet to make sure there were no wrinkles. Although she was still so young, she was accustomed to housework. Many of her foster parents forced her to do daily chores in exchange for food. If GiGi knew all she'd been through, she wouldn't dare ask her to help with making up a bed.

Picking up on how Rose didn't make eye contact with her, GiGi pried further. "Does Sam ever yell at your momma...or at you girls?" It may have been inappropriate to ask Rose such a question given her age, but the old bird didn't live by rules of civility. "You can tell me if he does, and I promise I won't tell."

Rose looked up at the woman who would soon be her grandmother. Tiny lines framed her eyes, giving hints of a lifetime filled with joy and laughter. GiGi didn't look her age. A size six, she sported designer duds and owned a closetful of stiletto heels. Her hair, formerly a dirty brown, was now highlighted with hues of soft baby blond. GiGi was beautiful… and funny…and Rose loved spending time with her. The girl would never say anything that might cause her not to be adopted. Rose had decided she needed GiGi in her life.

Shaking her head and scrunching her shoulders, Rose answered, "No, Sam never screams. He loves us." She chose to not confide in GiGi with the truth, but it didn't matter. Rose always lied when it suited her best interests. Telling the truth would change everything, and she wanted a stable home where GiGi was a part of her life.

Even though Viv often spoke about how difficult Rose and Ruby had been to parent, GiGi couldn't see it. To her, they were as perfect as her other grandkids. She was their grandma now, after all. Seizing an opportunity for giggles, GiGi picked up a pillow from the bed and threw it at Rose, popping her on the head.

Rose, in response, shot her a confused look. She'd obviously never been a part of a pillow fight and was unsure if she was in some sort of trouble.

Returning Rose's confused gaze with her own mischievous grin, GiGi picked up another pillow and threw it at the beautiful young biracial girl. "Wake up, silly goose. This is a pillow fight, and so far the old lady in the room is up by two."

Just as she picked up the third pillow, Rose caught on to the fun and picked up one of her own. Within seconds, the two were throwing pillows back and forth, laughing like two little girls. Tate, Ruby, and Miss Charity, upon hearing the gleeful noise, ran into the room and joined. Yes, it was clear, all the girls loved their GiGi.

When GiGi's husband, Poppy, stuck his head in the door to inform them Mary had arrived home, the girls quickly put the pillows back on the bed. "The eagle has landed with her bum ankle," GiGi announced, snickering, "so we better skedaddle outta here."

Rose and Ruby, wanting to please their grandma, immediately headed toward the bedroom door but stopped in their tracks when they felt a big thud on the back of their heads. GiGi was up to her typical antics.

"You girls have *got* to learn the rules to pillow fights," she said, laughing at the surprise on their faces when they turned to realize she was still throwing pillows. "A pillow fight ain't over till it's over."

Tate and Miss Charity were fully aware of GiGi's sneaky moves, so they'd kept their guard up. Rose and Ruby, however, were new to the whole "happy family" thing.

GiGi fell back on the bed as all the girls jumped on top of her, pounding her with pillows. Their laughter was pure gold. GiGi loved the girls as much as they loved her. "Uncle!" she cried, cackling. "You all win!"

Chapter 9

"How long are you planning to keep me here?"

Michael had asked the question every day since he'd been taken hostage by the maniacal Sam Smith, who believed he was following the commands of Yahweh. But Sam never answered. On this day, however, the bearded man seemed different. Was it a pep in his step, a half smile, or the fact that he was humming a tune? Michael couldn't put a finger on it.

Sam made a trip to his hunting cabin, way out somewhere in the woods, every day to feed Michael. The chains that kept him locked to the bed were long enough for him to make his way to the toilet and to sleep comfortably at night. A battery-operated tape recorder, kept out of reach in the main room, played two hours of sermons each day. Michael wished he could stomp on it. The cult was the reason he was now Sam's prisoner…the cult *and Viv.*

"Have you hurt Viv? Or the girls? Sam, you will eventually get caught, and you'll go to jail." Michael always pled with Sam to consider the consequences of the law. "It's not too late to make things right. If you'll let me go, give Viv a divorce, and leave town, I won't even press charges. This can all be kept between you and me."

Sam, on rare occasions when he'd answer Michael, simply spouted off scripture as if he were spewing tobacco juice. Most of the verses quoted were from the Old Testament regarding God's execution of judgment, but when confronted with Michael's comments about jail, he always quoted scripture about Paul and John, who had been put in jail for standing up for the cause of Christ. There was no getting to Sam. No emotion. No connection.

As Sam set up meals for that day, Michael continued to pepper him with questions. "You seem to be in a good mood today. Anything you wanna talk about?" Hoping for a hint of anything, the prisoner would never stop trying. Sam was known to be an avid hunter who enjoyed a good kill. Michael hoped to not end up dead.

"I really appreciate the food you bring me each day, Sam. Who taught you how to cook?" Michael, famished, dug into the mashed potatoes with gravy and asparagus that had been steamed with garlicky butter. He hoped showing appreciation might soften the heart of his captor.

As he chewed his food, he continued to babble. "Am I presumed to be dead? Have I had a proper funeral?" He added a slight laugh with the questions, just to keep the mood light. "I wonder who'd attend my funeral?" Keeping Sam calm was key to Michael's well-being and possibly to his survival.

*****

Bonnie was wealthy. She'd married well and had therefore divorced well. To allow Philip to live near his offspring, she'd purchased a home near Ocoee Street. They'd been living there together for the weeks leading up to the wedding date. This was the second home she'd owned in Cleveland, Tennessee, within walking distance of Mary. Before returning home after leaving the Coffey Barn, she made a stop by Mary's house, knowing she'd find Philip there.

"Well, well well…look at the bleached blond rat the cat dragged in," said GiGi, after opening the door to find Bonnie. "I assume you're here for Philip…but as you know, you're never welcome in my home." Trudy, hearing commotion at the front door, ran yapping toward Bonnie.

Bonnie hated GiGi nearly as much as she hated Mary, but she had a slight fondness for Trudy. They'd become buddies way back in the day when Bonnie was breaking into the old white house to steal from Mary and her family. Bending down to a squat, she patted her knee, and Trudy came running to her. "Good girl," she said, patting the miniature schnoodle on the head.

"Trader," GiGi mumbled.

In response, Bonnie flicked her blond locks from her face and stood, offering a death stare. "I wouldn't step one foot in your house if you begged me," she spat, allowing hate to rise.

"Since I won't be beggin' you, I guess you'll just have to priss your big plastic surgery–formed butt on over to your house and wait until the man who's *not* your husband is finished visiting with his actual family." Snickering obnoxiously as only she could, GiGi added, with a wave, "Ta ta, blondie!" before grabbing Trudy and closing the door in Bonnie's face.

As GiGi made her way back into the kitchen, Poppy asked who was at the front door. "Shh," she answered, giving him a wink of her eye.

Philip, who was in the bedroom tending to Mary, stuck his head out. "Who was that, GiGi?"

"Oh," she responded, "it was just a pizza delivery man who had the wrong house."

"Pizza sounds good," Philip quipped, "maybe I'll place an order for us."

GiGi, seeing she'd successfully skirted the truth, returned, "If you order it, I'll pay!"

*****

Michael had heard of Stockholm Syndrome but knew very little about it. He'd been held prisoner for a long time. He'd lost count of the days. With the windows covered, he had no way of distinguishing day from night. He knew, however, that his desire for Sam to stay with him and to carry on a conversation with him was not normal.

The depth of his loneliness was more than he'd ever experienced. Michael considered himself a people person, and not having any physical touch or conversation was taking a heavy toll. He'd heard of babies in orphanages who died from a lack of touch and could now understand how that was possible.

In the quiet of the days, he had time to think about his divorce and his brief affair with Viv. He'd always had a crush on Viv, and when he'd run into her at the local grocery, she'd reignited their old flame. It was as if no time had passed between them at all.

It's common for a man to be drawn to a damsel in distress, and Viv fit the bill. After he'd learned of the physical and emotional abuse she'd endured during her marriage to Sam, Michael had become her rescuer. He'd lost his own marriage when his wife had an affair with the contractor who had headed up the addition on their home. He needed to fill a void. Viv needed him even more. Michael wanted to feel needed.

As hours trudged slowly by each day, Michael could think of only Viv. He'd fallen in love once again with his high-school sweetheart. They were making plans on how they would be together, how she would escape from Sam's harmful grasp…and now he didn't even know what had happened with her. Did she believe Michael to be dead? Or had Sam killed her? His mind raced with the many possibilities. Not knowing was the toughest part of the ordeal.

As his captor left the cabin, Michael felt certain he noticed a change. And the change appeared to be a positive one, if that was possible given his situation. Even though Michael had been mentally preparing himself for the worst by not allowing himself to believe he would get out of his current situation alive, he began to allow a glimmer of optimism to enter his heart. Perhaps he would see Viv again. Maybe his dreams would come true.

Michael was right, of course. Unbeknownst to him, Bonnie Cutless had entered the equation. Everything had now changed.

Chapter 10

The adoption went through without a single snag. After spending fifteen minutes in a small room with a judge, papers were signed making Rose and Ruby the official daughters of Sam and Viv. As for Sam's part in the process, however, the adoption had nothing to do with love and everything to do with appeasing his religious philosophy. Once married, having children was the next step, which proved holiness, obedience, and favor.

His mind-set was backward. A new father should be reveling in the joy of creating a family unit, in the love that would be given and received, in all the teaching moments to come, and in the awesomeness of watching two human beings grow up to be all they're intended to be. Children should never be a check in a box. But that's precisely what Rose and Ruby were to Sam.

Not all who are abused will become abusers. Most all abusers, however, have been abused. It's a fact, and it's why defense attorneys fight so hard for the murderer, rapist, and child molester. It's why counselors, psychologists, and psychiatrists spend countless hours trying to help individuals dress up and cope with the skeletons in their closets. It's why pastors preach, why many teachers teach, and why prisons are filled to overflowing.

The world is an ugly place. Sin, unfortunately, isn't something that can be placed into a tidy box and put away. As long as abuse exists, there will be people who will fight for the abused who eventually become abusers themselves. Everyone deserves a shot at redemption, right? Even Sam.

As a child, Sam had a foot that turned in. Although a minor disability, it was significant enough to require a few years of leg braces and a specially-made shoe, enough to make him feel different. He'd never forgotten how embarrassed he was every time someone stared at his braces. It was the first thing people looked at. Instead of having friends, his peers had pitied him and treated him as someone who was less than themselves.

Once his foot finally straightened, it was no wonder Sam couldn't wait to prove himself. The boy loved baseball. It was a sport he and his father watched regularly on TV during the season, and they especially followed the Atlanta Braves. Sam dreamed, more often than anything else, that he'd one day be a part of that team.

As soon as his braces and special shoe were removed, Sam's dad bought him a baseball bat and glove. His dad was just as excited as he was. This wasn't only Sam's dream; this was the dream they'd dare to dream together.

Sam's first coach was outgoing, funny, and a superior athlete. He was also Sam's uncle, his mother's youngest brother. Determined and driven, Sam worked it out with his uncle to come to practice early and to stay late. Catching balls, practicing form, and learning every secret nuance of the game was a top priority for him. In the process, his uncle became his first real friend.

The abuse was subtle at first, which is fairly typical. The initial touch seemed accidental; in fact, his uncle was apologetic. He even appeared disconcerted and sheepish about it. As time passed, however, the touch became more frequent. It was awkward at first, but eventually, Sam started to look forward to it. It was just harmless touch, after all...nothing overtly sexual. Over time they also began viewing pornography together, and when Sam became a teenager, his uncle took him to his first show where he actually watched a sexual encounter between two adults.

"Sex is the most normal thing there is," his uncle had explained to him on countless occasions. "It was created by God, and there really are no rules as long as you appreciate the gift and enjoy it." His uncle was not only a coach, but a husband, father, and longtime pastor of a church. He was the finest man Sam had ever known. His uncle had died a few years before Sam married Viv, and he missed him. They'd always remained close and had always kept their secret between them.

When Sam turned on the computer and pulled up one of his favorite pornographic sites, he thought back to those times with his uncle. The experience hadn't impacted him in a negative way over the years. If anything, it was a positive experience. Didn't he recall enjoying the attention and the arousal? Perhaps those experiences with his uncle were the impetus that had allowed him to grow into a healthy sexual man. "Yep," he whispered to himself as he removed his boxer shorts, "I'm a man in every sense of the word." Taking a seat in his leather desk chair, Sam settled in, completely naked, to enjoy a time filled with fantasies that might cause even the most worldly of men to blush.

When he'd checked, Rose and Ruby were sound asleep. Viv had left early to meet her mother and sister for coffee, so the timing was perfect. What he didn't anticipate, though, was how Rose's chest had been rattling all night with the onset of a cold. When she walked into the room, he nearly fell out of his chair.

Chapter 11

Philip was dreaming about his wedding day, the one that didn't happen. In the dream, Bonnie was walking down the aisle toward him, wearing a flowing white gown. When Mary unexpectedly fainted, blocking Bonnie's path, Philip became startled. Bonnie, not able to react in time, tripped over Mary, falling…falling…falling…all in slow motion. And in the dream, Philip had to decide which woman to go to. Both were lying on the ground. Neither was moving. They were just there with their faces on the ground.

As he rushed toward them, still unsure which one to offer to help first, he broke from the dream because of Miss Charity. His youngest child was squealing with delight in the next room. His eyes fluttered.

It's an all-too-common reaction when one wakes in a familiar place. Barely opening his eyelids, he noticed the sunlight peeking through an opening in the full-length curtains. Rolling to his right, he reached out for Mary. "Mary," he said, his voice still gravely and low. And that's when it hit him. "Mary?" he yelled, rising up on his elbow while wiping drool from around his mouth. "What the…?"

Mary barely opened her eyes before shutting them again, returning to sleep. Philip immediately recalled Mary's injury…and simultaneously remembered that he'd left the wedding before marrying Bonnie and without saying good-bye to her. Now, he'd spent the night with Mary?

Before he could put much thought to it all, GiGi peeked her head into the room. "Philip, are you awake, dear?" she asked, honey dripping from her tongue. There was no way on earth Philip could ever fall privy to what she'd done. "I've made some breakfast," she whispered, so as to not wake Mary, "your favorite…blueberry pancakes."

The smile on her face seemed forced, and her eyes were open way too wide when she spoke. If he'd been paying attention, he would've noticed her expression mimicked those mannequins from the 70s that portrayed no reality whatsoever. Words were coming forth, and they were words he wanted to hear. Philip loved blueberry pancakes, and that knowledge was being utilized fully by the old bird. But behind the make-believe guise, this woman was guilt-laden, so her words were not attached to any honest emotion whatsoever. This was all phony.

What Philip didn't know was that Bonnie had left in a huff the night before. GiGi, keeping everyone busy, had made hot herbal tea for both Philip and Mary. She'd taken Philip to the side and asked him to stay with his ex-wife until she fell asleep while she and Poppy fed the dog, got Miss Charity and Tate off to bed, and cleaned the kitchen. The hospital had sent Mary home with some pain pills, and though Philip had offered to deal with his kids while GiGi and Poppy looked after Mary, GiGi had suggested that the pills might make Mary aggressive.

"Who knows how she might react to pain pills?" she'd asked, feigning alarm. "What if Mary becomes doped up, high as a kite, and agitated…and what if she tries to get up out of the bed to stand on that broken ankle? You're strong enough to work with her, Philip…Poppy and I are too old for that crap."

It had made perfect sense at the time. Since Mary wasn't one to swallow pills, GiGi had ground up her pain pill in the herbal tea. "She'll never taste it," she'd explained to Philip.

What he didn't know was that GiGi had also ground up half a pill in his tea. If Mary couldn't taste the pain pill, neither could Philip. Within minutes, the two were sound asleep on the bed together, just as the crafty schemer had planned.

Philip, still wearing his tuxedo pants, black socks, and a white T-shirt, stumbled out of bed. When he finally made his way into the kitchen, just as promised, he found blueberry pancakes awaiting him. Poppy, catching up on the latest news from his laptop while drinking a cup of coffee, glanced up for only a couple of seconds.

"Good mornin', Philip," he mumbled, and then went right back to scrolling. He presumed his wife had pulled some sort of stunt on an unsuspecting Philip, especially since she'd gone to the trouble to whip up pancakes for breakfast. As he figured, what he didn't know wouldn't hurt him. Don't ever ask what you don't want to know.

Philip took a seat. It was the chair he'd always sat in when he and Mary were married. It was his seat, wasn't it? "Good morning, Pops," he answered as GiGi placed a stack of pancakes in front of him. Having breakfast with his family felt normal. This was more normal than Philip could recall feeling in a long time.

"It's good to have you back home, sugar," GiGi said, her voice laced with a heavenly sort of joy. She patted him on his shoulder as she bent down to repeat in his ear, "This will always be your home." It did feel very much like home.

Glancing across the table at Miss Charity and Tate, who were grinning from ear to ear at the sight of their daddy at the table with them, he quickly guarded his pancakes with his arms. "Don't you girls even think about asking for a bite of *my* blueberry pancakes." Teasing his children was one of the things Philip missed most. His time with them now had been planned according to a schedule set by two lawyers who didn't give a twit about his daughters. While he and Mary worked well to maintain a healthy relationship with each other and to divide time with the girls as equally as possible, being with them daily was something he couldn't replace. Miss Charity, in response to her daddy's playfulness, flashed a mischievous grin and reached across the table with her hands, pretending to want to take the pancakes for herself.

"Oh, Miss Miss," he said, laughing, "you're daring to steal my pancakes, aren't you?"

The youngest Montgomery had not only been born with an extra chromosome and a heart defect, she remained nonverbal for the most part. Every once in a while, a word or two would slip out, but ever since the break-up of her family, she hadn't attempted to speak a single word. She was completely silent.

"You've messed with the wrong daddy now," Philip teased, "so now you'll have to deal with the tickle monster!"

Jumping up from his seat, he bounded around the table in a flurry of excitement, throwing his arms all around and stomping his feet. Just as he was tickling Miss Charity, causing her to giggle with complete abandon, Mary hobbled into the room on crutches.

"What are you doing here?" she asked, clearly con-fused. "And…did you sleep in my bed with me last night?"

GiGi, standing nearby, cleared her throat and sang, "Mary, would you like some blueberry pancakes?"

Chapter 12

Philip felt a bit chagrined when he finally arrived at the house he'd been sharing with Bonnie. How in God's name would he ever explain bolting from the wedding and staying out all night without calling her? Opening the door, an envelope was lying in the floor at his feet.

She was gone. Bonnie had packed all her things during the night and was gone. The note didn't say where she was going. It simply stated that she was making a break from him, and that though she'd tried to be all he wanted and needed, she could see his unwavering loyalty would always be to Mary.

The charming little bungalow house in the historic district of downtown Cleveland, Tennessee, had been built in 1928 and carefully restored to its original state at the direction of Bonnie. Making his way to the screened in sleeping porch, Philip sat upon the custom-made hanging daybed and considered his predicament. The wedding now ironically seemed far behind him. The evening spent with Mary had changed everything.

As the large ceiling fan above him blew a gentle breeze of air against his face, he considered how he should feel—a twinge of alarm or sadness?—but instead, he felt relief. Bonnie was gone. Philip hadn't married her. There was still hope for he and Mary to be together again.

*****

When Bonnie arrived at the cabin, she was shocked to see Michael chained to a bed. She'd met Sam at a gas station in town and had followed him out into the middle of nowhere. The cabin was not even on a road; there was no way anyone would ever find it.

"OK, Sam," she said, her eyes boring into the man who'd been at the center of a missing person's hullaballoo in town, "I see you've left one tiny detail out of our discussions." She couldn't believe it. What did Michael have to do with their plan? While she'd never met the man, Bonnie immediately recognized him from all the media attention his sudden disappearance had drawn. "Everyone in town thinks you're dead, Michael," she added, careful to not let him detect any hesitation on her part.

"Well, obviously, he ain't dead," responded Sam, looking toward Michael with disgust, "but I wish I'd gone ahead and killed him the night I caught him trespassing on my property."

Michael remained silent. The fact that someone else now knew about his terrible predicament meant his chances of survival had just increased. To his recollection, he'd never seen the woman before but was counting on her having a more nurturing, tender nature than Sam. Unfortunately, he was wrong.

"He was trespassing on your property?" she asked while exploring the small cabin. "So, you kidnapped him?" Laughing, she added, "That's interesting."

As Sam filled Bonnie in on more details, including Michael's affair with Viv, Michael sat like a stone, not moving…not showing any emotion. Unsure how to play the current shift in dynamics in his favor, he decided his best maneuver was to not play at all.

"Oh my," teased Bonnie, making her way over to the bed and plopping down hard next to Michael. "It looks like you chose the wrong woman to mess around with."

Michael's face expressed nothing. The woman's mouth was only inches from his, but he clinched his mouth and remained melancholy. Bonnie laughed. "Sam, honey, you may have those rugged, rough-around-the-edges good looks, but Michael is dreamy." Running her fingers through the prisoner's hair, she asked, "How long has it been since you've been with Viv? You know, in a sinful way?"

Michael continued to hold his ground. Barely blinking his eyes, he stared into Bonnie's baby blues. This fiasco was no longer about him, but Viv. If she and Sam were talking about her, she was still very much alive. He had to return to her and protect her from this monster. He had to save Rose and Ruby too.

Turning away from Michael for just a moment, Bonnie leaned her elbow back on the bed to address Sam. "Could you hand me my purse, handsome?" she asked.

Sam wasn't thrilled about the way Bonnie was flirting with Michael, and his attitude showed it. He picked up her purse and threw it at her.

"Rawr!" she yelped, catching the purse in her arms as it hit her in the chest. "It looks like Sam's a tad jealous of you, Michael."

Rummaging through her purse, Bonnie finally found a small red pouch. She unzipped it and pulled out a needle. Holding it in her fingers, she pulled it up even with her eyes and turned back toward Michael. The needle was now between them, dead even with their noses, as they looked at one another, eye to eye.

"Do you like to play games?" she asked, grinning from ear to ear. "Let's see," she teased, "I think I'm gonna call this game 'tell Bonnie the truth or get a needle pushed up under your fingernails.'"

Michael smiled. The visitor's name was Bonnie.

*****

Philip sat swinging on the hanging outdoor bed, dreaming of how he'd work his way back into the old white house with his family. That's where he belonged. Until then, he'd pack his things and move back into the makeshift apartment he'd built at his office. Just as he was about to stand up and start packing, he heard a voice.

"Well, hotshot, what's your plan now?" she asked, peering through the screen.

Not expecting anyone, he nearly jumped out of his skin. "Good Lord!" he cried. "You scared the fool out of me."

GiGi giggled. "Good! I'm about sick and tired of you being a fool." Pushing her way through the hedge, she planted her face against the screen, trying to get a better look beyond the sleeping porch and into the house. "Is the she-devil at home?" she asked, her voice barely above a whisper.

*****

"How are you going to measure whether I'm telling the truth or not?" Michael asked as he involuntarily shivered. The threat of a needle being stabbed beneath his fingernails was getting to him.

Bonnie, taking the needle between her right first finger and thumb, pushed it up under the first finger on her left hand until she bled. "I'll just know," she answered, placing her bleeding nail into her mouth and sucking.

A bit unhinged by the quagmire he was in, Michael decided to tell the absolute truth…no matter what Bonnie asked him and no matter the impact his honesty might have on Sam. "All right then, ask away," he said, with resignation, knowing there was no possible way he'd escape the needle. "I'll be brutally honest and tell you whatever you want to know."

Bonnie asked many questions. Parts of her query were embellished with benign vanity, such as, "Do you think I'm beautiful?" or "What do you think it would be like to have sex with me?" Michael about fell over when she pulled up her shirt to flash her see-through lacy bra and asked, "Do you prefer full breasts like mine or itty bitty breasts like Viv?" He received a puncture wound for that answer.

Most of her questions, however, had a direct bearing on the kidnapping. She asked details about his brief affair with Viv, his feelings for her, and his intentions. As he answered each question, he made sure to keep his focus solely on Bonnie. While Sam was in the room, Michael didn't want to look into the eyes of the husband of his lover. Guilt played no hand in the matter. Every decision hinged on survival.

A few outlier questions were about Mary and her death dreams. That stumped him. Although Michael had been vaguely informed by Viv on the matter, the truth was that they spoke very little about outside family matters. Most of their time had been selfishly spent on themselves.

He had to wonder about those questions. What did Mary's mental issues have to do with his love affair with Viv? What were Sam and Bonnie up to?

Chapter 13

Rose and Ruby were with Mary. Viv, busy working with a future bride on wedding plans, had dropped them off for a few hours. Everyone in the family had noticed a profound change in Viv over the previous months, so Mary was happy to help out whenever an opportunity presented itself.

To all who loved her, Viv had always been hoity-toity. While her southern snark was at times over-bearing, her heart was as good as gold. Lately, however, she'd become withdrawn and moody. Mary and GiGi had tried to get her to open up about the sudden change in her behavior, but Viv main-tained that she was feeling overwhelmed because of the addition of Rose and Ruby, along with her new blossoming wedding business.

"I've just taken in two hooligan kids while holding down two jobs," she'd said. "Wouldn't you expect me to be tired and moody?"

It made sense. During the day, she worked as a mobile therapist for differently abled students in several local schools and on weekends was knee deep in weddings. With the recent adoption of two young girls, it was no wonder she wasn't feeling her usual self. It didn't stop her mother and sister from worrying though. And it definitely didn't stop them from peppering her with questions.

At a tipping point, Viv had harshly expressed how their barrage of concern left her feeling even more on edge. She demanded that they let it go and allow her to work through the adjustment on her own timetable. Not wanting to alienate themselves from her, both had agreed to give her space but had suggested she give up one of the jobs so she could spend more time caring for herself and getting to know her new daughters.

That had offended her. "Are we returning to the forties and fifties?" she'd asked. "Why don't I just stay home to be a momma and let Sam be the breadwinner?" At that point, Mary and GiGi decided to never bring up the subject again. GiGi was in a quandary. She'd never thought of Viv as one who'd be unduly concerned about success in the workplace. Both her daughters were losing their minds.

*****

With all the grandparents out for the evening at a church social event, Mary had Rose, Ruby, Tate, and Miss Charity all to herself. They'd made mini meatloafs, mashed potatoes, sautéed broccoli, and chocolate cupcakes with sprinkles. Just as they sat down to dig in, Viv called to check in.

"We're getting ready to fill our bellies to the brim," Mary answered, grinning at the girls, who surrounded her at the dining table. "And after dinner, we're going to work on a craft project and then watch a movie, so just take your time."

Viv had seemed pleased to hear that Mary had her daughters covered for the evening. She needed time away from them and from Sam. Even though juggling two jobs was tiring, it did give her a break.

After ending the call and placing the phone on the table, Mary told Rose and Ruby that their momma had sent her love. She noticed how her words seemed to please them. Even though they were still little girls, they clearly understood how everyone was trying to make their transition into the family as seamless as possible. "Now, who's gonna pray for this scrumptious food tonight before we dig in?"

Miss Charity, being nonverbal, bowed her head and placed her hands delicately up under her chin. She was ready. The quicker they got to praying, the quicker she got to eat the food. The kid may have had special needs, but she was sharp as a tack.

"I will," shouted Ruby, raising her hand. Rose, not too keen on faith and God, shot her sister a sideways glance, but Ruby ignored it. "Can I pray?" she asked, "Pleeeeaaaase, Aunt Mary?"

Tate, a young teenager now, was surrounded by young girls who were full of silly energy. "Nope, I'm praying tonight," she said, playfully badgering Ruby. She missed her big brother more than anyone could comprehend. It was good for her to be surrounded by her newly adopted cousins. They kept her company and enjoyed playing with her. Mary's middle child was a treasure. Tate had a soft nature and always worked to make everyone happy. "We're having meatloaf and mashed potatoes, which was prepared by you girls," she said, "so I think I need to pray over it just to make sure I don't die of food poisoning."

Rose and Ruby burst out in giggles. "We washed our hands, Tater!" they said, laughing. "And we're very good cooks, right Aunt Mary?"

Miss Charity still sat quietly, waiting with her hands folded beneath her chin. Though she had no words, her actions spoke loud and clear. These goofy girls were keeping her from digging into her food. The kid was hungry.

Mary rolled her eyes, "OK, girls," she said, acting agitated but feeling as happy as she could recall feeling in a long time. "Since I did see Rose and Ruby wash their hands, and since I know they are indeed the best cooks in the county, I don't think we have to worry about food poisoning."

Rose and Ruby craned their necks toward Tate and grinned. "Did you hear that?" asked Rose. "Your momma says we are the best cooks in the county."

Tate grinned. Wills used to tease her mercilessly. Now it was her time to be the one who teased. The role reversal gave her some comfort. Ruby was seated in Wills's chair. She imagined him there, closed her eyes, bowed her head, and prepared her heart for the prayer.

"So," Mary said, "I'm going to choose Ruby to say our prayer."

It was fitting.

Ruby clasped her hands together and tucked them beneath her chin. "Dear God," she said, her voice gentle and true, "thank you for my new family. I love GiGi, Aunt Mary, and Tater very, very much. Thank you for keeping me and Rose safe. Thank you for this meatloaf because I've never had meatloaf before and it looks really good…and especially thank you for the chocolate cupcakes with sprinkles." Opening her eyes to peek up toward Miss Charity, who she'd watched being abused by Sam, she added, "And one more thing, God. Please protect Miss Charity with your big strong hands because she needs you more than the rest of us do. Amen."

Mary, completely thrown by the tenderness of the moment, had to fight back tears. "Amen," she agreed, sniffling. "Now, girls, let's eat."

*****

The truth was that Viv was battling major depression. Her brief affair with Michael had ended with a gunshot she'd heard through her cell phone. Her life had changed forever in that moment, but she couldn't tell anyone.

Mary had been so crazy with her death dreams and had shown up with reservations to a girl's weekend away at a fancy hotel out of town that fateful night. She'd dropped Miss Charity off for Sam to babysit without telling anyone of her plans. He was already looking after Rose and Ruby, but Viv had a strong hunch that he might be abusive toward the one bearing an extra chromosome. Abusers abuse.

No one knew about the affair Viv had had with Michael. The two had managed to keep it a complete secret. Michael had been her one true love. They'd dated in high school, and even though their relationship ended, she'd never stopped loving him. He'd married, but Viv hadn't found anyone who could replace Michael. Up into her thirties, she'd remained single until Sam came along with his lies. Looking back on their brief courtship, she'd fallen for the lies, not for Sam. The two were poles apart on so many levels.

The abuse with Sam had started immediately after their wedding. Viv had never been subjected to anything like it in her life and didn't know how to handle it. She kept thinking if she'd change, maybe Sam would change too. But nothing worked. The more she ignored his behavior, the more violent the behavior became.

Her castle in the air showed up unexpectedly, however, the day she ran into Michael in the grocery store. Not only did fireworks go off in her heart, but her world stopped long enough for her to realize what she wanted and needed in life. The abuse no longer mattered. Viv felt alive once again. And when Michael explained that he was recently divorced, Viv's future was wide open again. She'd move heaven and earth if needed to be with him.

On the night of Michael's disappearance, as she was escaping with Mary for that getaway weekend, she'd asked him to go to her home to see if he saw or heard any evidence that would lead him to believe Miss Charity could be in danger. As he carefully lurked around the house, concerned for the well-being of not only Miss Charity, but of Rose and Ruby, who'd also been left in Sam's care, he kept Viv on the phone. She could hear his footsteps, the rhythm of his breaths…and then, Sam's voice.

Sam and Michael had a brief confrontation with words before she heard a gunshot. It was all her fault. What was worse, Sam refused to tell Viv whether he'd injured Michael, scared him away, or killed him. The unknown was killing her.

Every day she carried her phone with the ringer on, hoping for a call or text from Michael. But the call never came. With each new day, the darkness loomed closer and closer to Viv. It was enveloping her...smothering her.

She wanted to go to the police to tell them every-thing she knew, but Sam had threatened to kill her and her family if she did. Did he mean it? She didn't know, but after hearing that gunshot, she didn't want to take any chances.

Sam was the type of man who was capable of any-thing if he felt he was backed up to a wall with noth-ing to lose. Her hope of keeping her family safe and of possibly seeing Michael again hinged on keeping Sam stable. That much Viv knew. So she pressed on, playing the game and bearing Sam's abuse.

Chapter 14

Mary had just finished getting the last of the little girls out of the bathtub when Philip showed up. A couple of weeks had passed since the wedding that never happened, and he'd made a visit to the old white house every day since that fateful day under the auspices of checking on Mary's injury. With each visit, Philip also brought a small gift of some sort, and this particular evening, he brought an iced mocha latte. It was her favorite.

Wearing a pair of gym shorts with a simple white T-shirt and gray Nike skateboarding shoes, Philip stood in Miss Charity's doorway and watched as Mary pulled a pink nightgown over their youngest daughter's curly wet hair. Even after all the years they'd known each other, as Mary gazed up at him holding her much needed caffeine, she felt a familiar flutter in her tummy. He'd been so good to look after her. So tender.

"Whatcha got there, Chief?" she asked, half flirting.

Miss Charity, following her mother's eyes toward her daddy, took off in a sprint and wrapped her arms around one of his legs. In response, he bent down to kiss the top of her head. The youngest Montgomery instinctively patted the spot where her dad had planted a smooch. She adored him.

"I've got an idea," Mary suggested, rising up from her knees to meet him. "Why don't you take little Miss Miss, and I'll take the latte?" Snatching the coffee, she winked her eye and hobbled out of the room on her boot cast, leaving her ex-husband behind in a clunky wake.

"Oh, no you didn't!" he yelped, scooping Miss Charity up onto his hip and taking off after Mary. "At the very least, you could say thank you…or a kiss on the cheek would suffice too, if you're interested."

A chase ensued; flirting was fueling it all. Miss Charity giggled as she and her daddy zoomed out of the room behind Mary, badgering her relentlessly. Mary loved the banter. It had always been her favorite part of their relationship.

"A kiss?" Mary asked, scoffing with laughter, still thudding through the house. "You move way too fast for me, Chief," she teased.

She'd called him Chief. Philip's heart soared when he heard the love name that only Mary was allowed to use. "Too fast?" he yelled. "We've known each other for a hundred years!"

Still scooting through the house, hobbling with all her might, Mary looked back over her shoulder. "Are you calling me old? Because if you are, that will get you nowhere!"

She was quick-witted. Beautiful. And possibly the best mother in the world. Philip suddenly felt a pain of regret as he considered how close he was to shutting the door on their love story. Ending the chase, he took the lead and turned to face her. "You are forever young in my eyes, Mare Bear," he said, his voice gentle and kind. "You were my very first kiss, and I am hoping against hope that you'll be my last."

For the first time in a long time, hope rose up in Mary and took her breath away. She felt it. She welcomed it. And she dared to wish that she was not dead and not in a death dream.

*****

Viv showed up early to her meeting with the future bride. They'd decided on a sandwich shop just on the outskirts of town so both could have a quick bite to eat while they discussed colors, style, and a price range.

This was Viv's least favorite part of the process. First meetings, from her recent experiences, were typically a waste of time. Future brides, in the beginning stages of wedding planning, were such romantics—and their budgets didn't often meet their expectations. This meeting would be a fluff meeting. It would be her job to cut the fat.

There was a day and time when a wedding planner was able to enjoy working with a bride who had dreamed her entire life about the big day when she'd say "I do." In the process of planning, that bride might thumb through some bridal magazines and visit a few florists and bridal shops, but the primary focus was on how she and her future husband would say vows that would unite them for the rest of their lives. Of course the vintage bride wanted the venue to be presentable, reverent, and special, but her wedding day was not meant to be a spectacle.

Nowadays, however, brides were much more demanding and unrealistic. With the advent of television shows that promote brides outdoing one another, teamed up with social media sites that offer twenty-four-hour-a-day fantastical advice and ideas, the modern bride was under pressure to create a one-of-a-kind affair that would be seared into the minds of her guests for all time. Weddings were no longer about two people becoming one but about an experience.

As Viv sat pondering the dread, she barely noticed a blonde with a ponytail sleeked back into a red ball cap walk into the small eatery. Dressed in black leggings and a red T-shirt, the woman made her way over to Viv and sat down. When Viv looked up, she couldn't believe her eyes. "Bonnie, what the heck are you doing here?"

*****

The kids had been bathed and dressed for bed and were watching a movie inside a makeshift fort Philip had prepared with blankets and chairs. Tate, in the middle of the busy brood of girls, held a large bowl of buttered popcorn in her lap, doling it out as each hand reached out for another piece.

"Viv should be here by now, shouldn't she?" asked Philip as he and Mary sat at the kitchen table. "I would think that Sam would've called by now looking for her and the girls."

Mary was thinking the same thing but quickly explained how Viv's behavior had been strange since the adoption of Rose and Ruby. "She says they're constantly instigating mischief and discord in her home and that it causes great stress in her life, but GiGi and I haven't seen it," she said, trying to make sense of the shift in her sister's personality. "She drops them off here with us often, and we've not had any issues with them at all."

Philip had known Mary's family for most all his life and immediately offered a solution. "Well," he said, "she's either depressed, hormonal, or having an affair."

Mary looked at him like he had ten heads. "Viv, having an affair? With those skirts down to her ankles and that dinky doily on her head?" She laughed. "You've lost it."

His eyebrows were raised, and then she recalled that he was speaking from experience. "OK, so I do see how your behavior changed when you were hooking up with Bonnie…but Viv just wouldn't go there."

His eyebrows raised even higher. He was right. She would've bet the bank on Philip, that he'd never cheat. But in a moment of weakness, he did cheat on her. And during that time, he was a completely different person.

"All I'm saying," he offered, holding a coffee cup in his hand and bringing it up to his lips, "is that she is out very late tonight, and that is suspicious." Taking a sip, he placed the cup back down on the table. "Now, what do you say we go join that gaggle of giggling geese in the fort for the rest of the movie?"

Standing he made his way over to Mary. "Don't worry too much because you have your own problems to deal with." He laughed, knocking on her boot cast with his knuckles. Squatting down to the floor with his back turned to her, he instructed, "Climb up on my back, Cowgirl. It's time for the chief to take you for a ride."

Mary, quite caught up in Philip, did as he asked. She climbed upon his back as he galloped around the house, whinnying like a real thoroughbred. For a moment, both forgot they were divorced. Tate peeked outside the fort and was so happy to see at least one part of her life coming back together.

How long had it been since she'd seen her big brother? She couldn't even remember. But for that blip of time, her parents were happy again. Sitting back in the fort, she giggled.

"What's going on with your parents?" asked Rose, popping a piece of popcorn in her mouth.

"Nothing at all," Tate answered. "Things are perfect."

*****

Viv was stunned to see Bonnie Cutless. Everyone expected the rejected bride to be out of town, working on how she'd spin the whole wedding debacle to make herself the victim of all victims. She'd ridden Viv like a rail during the short planning process, not to mention the fact that she'd tried to marry her sister's soul mate. Viv literally despised the woman.

"I'd love to sit and chat with you, Bonnie," she said, "but I'm waiting on a bride who is meeting me here to begin the planning process of her wedding."

The condescension wasn't lost on Bonnie, who fired back, "Let me guess. Her name is Julie, she's marrying Brad, and they want a barn wedding next June," she said, with a grin. "It's just a hunch, of course, but I'm super anxious to find out…" Bonnie cleared her throat to give the weight of the information time to settle in. "Did I get it right, Viv?"

Bonnie had given her an earful. As the truth began to dawn on Viv, that she'd been set up by Bonnie, the fact that she was dealing with a crazy person also occurred to her. Quickly looking around the room, Viv spotted the exit door and made a mental note of each face in the room.

"Could you hand me your phone, Viv?" Bonnie asked, reaching out her hand.

Viv had the phone in her hand and gripped it tighter.

"C'mon, be a good girl and give Bonnie your cell phone."

"What's wrong with you?" asked Viv. "Not only will I not hand you my phone, but I'm leaving." Digging a five-dollar bill out of her purse, she placed it on the table to pay for the sweet tea she'd been served. "If this was supposed to be some sort of joke, it's not funny." Viv pushed her chair away from the table, flung her purse over her shoulder, and was just about to stand.

"Give me your phone, and I'll take you to Michael."
Bonnie not only had a straight flush, she held the
whole deck of cards.

Chapter 15

GiGi and Poppy were having a lively time at the church social. Philip's parents, Pip and Aggie, were in attendance as well, so GiGi's primary concern was that she and Poppy upstage them. On this particular evening, the competition was over stewed meat, tomatoes, onions, and beans.

The pastor and his wife, Preacher Walker and Jeannie, were the hosts and had arranged the parameters of the chili cook-off. The entrants had to make everything from scratch as a couple, provide their recipe, and make enough to feed ten people. With twelve hopeful competitors, there was enough chili to feed a small army.

As fate would have it, the judges narrowed the final two competitors down to Pip and Aggie and GiGi and Poppy. While everyone gathered at long tables to dig into the chili feast, the judges went into a back room to deliberate. The wait was driving GiGi batty.

"I don't even know why this is a competition at all if it has come down to us and those two numbskulls," she chanted, not trying to be discreet with her true feelings. "After all, Poppy and I have been long-term members of this congregation, while Pip and Aggie just popped back in trying to horn their way into our affairs after deciding to finally become grandparents."

Many of the ladies at the table nodded in agreement with GiGi. She'd been a stalwart force for years in their church, making dinners for new moms, arranging visits for the homebound, and attending every funeral without exception. She arrived at church early and was typically one of the last to leave. If GiGi was anything at all, she was a died-in-the-wool Baptist, saved by the blood of the Lamb.

"Now hold on for just a minute," chided Poppy, daring to chime in with an opposing view. "Pip retired, and he and Aggie have chosen to move here full time now to be a part of their grandkids' lives. It wasn't that they didn't want to be present for their grandchildren all these years, it was that a job took them away from our city."

GiGi nearly choked on a chili bean. "I can't believe you would defend those sidewinders," she said, her eyes rolling into the back of her head. "Wild horses couldn't drag me away from this fine city, my beloved church, my dear friends, and especially my grandchildren. Money is the root of all evil, and it was the mighty dollar that bewitched the two of them—but not me. For me, family will always come first."

She was laying it on thick, nodding her head as she spoke, and the women at the table were buying into every word she spoke. The truth was that none of them appreciated Aggie and Pip's intrusion into their inner circle. GiGi, prissy and bossy, was not always easy to deal with. Aggie, however, was eccentric and snooty. There was a difference.

"It was a job transfer," corrected Poppy. "Pip transferred with his company to another city because they offered him a promotion…that's hardly a slam against the grandkids."

But GiGi had an audience and was clearly on a roll; she wouldn't be moved on her opinion by her husband or anyone else. "Well, while I've been here takin' care of my grandchildren since birth, waitin' on them hand and foot, wipin' their snotty noses, and supportin' all their extracurricular activities, Pip and Aggie have been off doin' their own thing. And now, when they're getting old as dirt, they pop back into town expecting us all to roll out the red carpet, and I'm not about to do it."

GiGi had her posse, a longtime group of loyal friends who would take her side even if they believed her side to be wrong. Aggie, who'd not been in town very long, had already formed her own group of friends. GiGi called them groupies because they fawned over Aggie, hanging on her every word and complimenting her style. So while

GiGi sat ripping into Aggie, the same was being done to her at a nearby table.

"We're in church, Aggie," Pip scolded. "Shouldn't you demonstrate grace and mercy?"

"To that old bat? Never!" responded Aggie. "GiGi acts like she owns this church, waltzing around in her high heels like she's the Queen of Sheba. Well, the last time I checked, this church belonged to Jesus."

The women on Aggie's side of the line agreed wholeheartedly. One even shouted an "Amen!" while another added a "Glory!" Their vocal support only encouraged the venom to flow.

"Just you wait and see," Aggie said. "I'm going to win this chili cook-off and prove that I'm a contender in this town."

It was pointless. GiGi and Aggie would never find common ground. And pitting them against one another in any type of competition only proved to rile them up into even more of a feverish furor.

When Preacher Walker finally took the microphone to announce the winner, he took a deep breath. The results were not going to make either happy, and he knew it. "It's a tie," he said, feigning happiness. "The judges said both women created the best chili they'd ever tasted. It was too close to call."

GiGi, aghast, rose to her feet and shouted, "A tie, my eye! I've given blood, sweat, and tears to this church, and Aggie pops in on a wing and a prayer—yet we're judged as equals? I don't think so." Placing her hands on her hips, GiGi stood her ground firmly. "I demand a recount, a tiebreaker, a taste-off…or whatever we need to do to make sure I'm the winner of this thing."

In response, Preacher Walker's eyes just about bugged out of his head. Scratching his neck nervously with his eyebrows raised, he said: "GiGi, I know this is disturbing, but like I already said…it was just too close to call."

"I say that you be the one to break the tie, Preacher. Somebody get him a bowl of my chili and a bowl of Aggie's chili." The old bird's eyes shone a glint of mischief as she placed unexpected pressure on her pastor. "He is not only a man of God, but he knows good chili. Who's with me?"

The crowd of people, not knowing exactly what to do—but definitely not wanting to cross GiGi—clapped their hands, applauding the suggestion.

Aggie, fuming to the point where she was just about ready to explode, stood to her feet. She raised her hands to steal away their attention. "Listen," she said, her voice raised, "I'll just give the win to GiGi. In the name of Jesus, I am turning the other cheek and offering mercy because I don't believe the Good Lord cares about winning as much as he cares about our desire to be a good neighbor."

The room fell silent as the eyes of the parishioners darted back and forth between the two archenemies.

"Love thy neighbor as thyself," she said. "That's what I'm doing today. I'm following the Good Book. So without further ado, GiGi, I'd like to offer my congratulations." Raising her plastic cup to the sky, which was filled with sweetened iced tea, she offered a toast. "Here's to the winner of this year's chili cook-off!"

Preacher Walker, feeling a sudden rush of relief, quickly picked up the six-inch-tall trophy that sported a silver spoon, and ran it over to GiGi's table. But just before he could reach her, she shouted, "Hold up! You just hold onto your horses, Preacher, 'cause I don't accept!"

There was probably no one on earth who knew GiGi's weaknesses as well as Aggie, because even though they despised one another, they were more alike than two peas in a pod. It was as plain as day to Gigi. Aggie wasn't being gracious to her, because that would be an impossibility. Instead, she was being holier than thou.

"This is the South, Aggie, and as you know, that hogwash don't fly down here," GiGi added, directing her pent-up anger toward her nemesis. "This is a competition, and I'm gonna win it fair and square, or I'm not gonna win it at all."

Aggie, knowing how GiGi would respond, spontaneously grinned. If she'd tried to withhold her smile, her face might've cracked under the strain. But she didn't try. She smiled the biggest smile she could muster. "Preacher Walker, since GiGi has turned down that trophy, bring it over here to me…because I accept."

What had just happened? GiGi had been outfoxed. What could Preacher Walker do? He looked between both women, back and forth, and realized he had no choice. He had offered the trophy to GiGi, and she had rejected it, so he did the only thing he could do. He handed the trophy to Aggie.

Chapter 16

An angel stood regally by Viv's side. Invisible to everyone in the room, his presence could've been felt by Viv had she been more spiritually aware. When she was much younger, she'd been much more perceptive. It's that way with the human race.

Viv's angel had been with her since the day she was born. As he stood guard, considering her current dilemma, memories of her younger days flooded his thoughts. She'd always been feisty, had not always been the best judge of character, but had a heart as pure as gold. He earnestly loved her.

One memory in particular stood out to him above all others. It was when she and Mary had drawn a line with a marker down the middle of their shared bedroom and had declared themselves no longer sisters. During that time, they didn't speak to one another, refused to share a bathroom, and scheduled days of the week when each would eat alone at the dinner table with their parents so they wouldn't have to eat together. It was a crazy time for the family.

GiGi was just as strong willed at that time, and though she tried her level best to force the girls to reunite, they refused. She threatened, bribed, and begged, but they wouldn't budge. They wouldn't even ride to school together. Viv, determined not to ride in the car with her "former sister," started catching the school bus.

Mary, a social butterfly and free spirit, was always more popular and well-liked than Viv. As a result, she had more friends, and they took her side over Viv's. Within days of their very public fight, the majority of the school was shunning Viv. At that time, Mary saw it as a victory and relished in it. Viv, meanwhile, felt rejected and hurt.

As the angel thought back on the memory, he placed his hand upon Viv's shoulder and recalled the many prayers Viv had prayed during that time. She'd repented of her anger toward Mary and had asked the Lord to heal their broken relationship. As his mind settled back to the moment when everything changed, a soft smile swept across his face.

In the middle of the day, just after lunch, Mary walked down the school hallway when she heard a group of girls verbally bullying her sister. They were telling Viv that she would never be as pretty or as popular as Mary. They called her a loser.

When Mary saw the look on her sister's face and heard what the girls were saying, she instinctively took off in a full sprint to stand by Viv's side.

"No, please stop," she told them, grabbing hold of her sister in a full hug. "This whole fight with Viv is my fault. She's the best sister in the world." Mary's eyes filled with tears. "I'm so sorry, Viv," she said. "You can't listen to them. You are so very beauti-ful...do you hear me? You are my beautiful sister."

As both sisters stood in the hall that day, they wept tears filled with love and forgiveness. And from that moment on, they always had each other's backs. They were a team. Although they still argued like typical siblings do, their bond was unbreakable. God had used something negative and turned it into something very good.

*****

Viv, still confused about what kind of information Bonnie had about Michael, answered, "No, Bonnie, I'm not giving you my phone and I'm certainly not going anywhere with you tonight."

Viv's head was spinning. To her knowledge, Bonnie had never met Michael...and she had no way of knowing about Viv's connection to Michael. The whole situation was making her feel physically ill.

"Let me explain this to you so you'll understand," Bonnie whispered, leaning across the table so Viv could see the seriousness in her face. "This isn't just about your cell phone or Michael, sweetheart... it's about Mary too. You either come with me, or Mary dies."

Viv was stupefied. None of this made sense. "Mary?" she asked. "You're going to kill my sister?"

*****

Viv's angel, though he hadn't been made privy to all that his charge would be facing, knew without a doubt that she was in the care of her Maker and that all would turn out for her good and for His glory. As he studied the face of Bonnie, he saw so much heartache and pain. Perhaps this was all for her salvation. He didn't know. His job was to stay by Viv's side, and he wouldn't let her down.

As Viv pushed away from the table and began to stand, he noticed her hands trembling. She was frightened. The angel stood behind her. Placing his hands on her arms, he helped her to stand. "I'm here," he whispered in her ear, hoping to offer her some peace.

When she walked toward the door to leave, following behind Bonnie, the appointed angel walked by her side. Long, wavy brown hair paired with hulking features made him a force that most humans would fear. His piercing green eyes, however, showed a gentleness that could calm a newborn baby. "Stand tall," he said, his voice resolute and reassuring. "God is on your side."

She couldn't physically hear his words, but her spirit seized them. And she stood straighter, with her head held high. "Lord help me," she mumbled, digging deep for a morsel of faith, trying to stave off all fear.

In response, her angel grinned. He'd taught her well. When in need, just call out to the Lord using whatever words come to mind. Like the mighty waves that crash upon the tender shore, He's always there.

Chapter 17

GiGi was fired up on the way home from the chili cook-off. Poppy said very little because he knew whatever he said would immediately turn into a war of words. Aggie had double-crossed his bride, and she'd never taken being double-crossed very well.

"I looked like a big boob tonight, Pops," she stated, shaking her head. The thought of Aggie getting the best of her in front of all of her church peers was driving her up the wall.

He said nothing.

"This calls for revenge…an eye for an eye…tit for tat…whatever you want to call it," she added. "And it's gonna be a whopper whenever I come up with my strategy."

Still, Poppy said nothing. It would be a no-win situation for him, and he knew it.

GiGi, upon realizing she was having a conversation with herself, attempted to engage him. "Hello? Husband that I pledged my ever-lovin' life to, are you with me on this?"

He nodded his head.

"So, you do believe Aggie needs a dose of her own poison?" she asked.

Again, he nodded his head. The man was too afraid to speak. Years of living with a type-A personality that could leave all the world's leaders stumbling in her wake had taught him that silence is indeed golden.

Her cell phone buzzed. He silently prayed a prayer of thanks to God. For a few minutes, at least, he was off of her radar.

*****

Viv had handed her phone over to Bonnie, and the two were on their way to an undisclosed location. As they drove on in the night, Viv was concerned about what she'd agreed to. Why did Bonnie need her phone? And where were they going?

"Are you taking me to see Michael?" she asked, wondering how Bonnie Cutless knew anything at all about her lover.

Bonnie said nothing. She had what she was after, which was power over Viv. She'd deliver her to Sam, and in turn, Sam would deliver Mary to her.

*****

"No, Mare Bear, I haven't heard one word from Viv or Sam," GiGi said, sounding happy as a clam on the phone with Mary. She'd just been raising Cain about Aggie but managed to put it all aside as if the chili cook-off had never swayed in the favor of the one she despised. "Have you tried calling them?"

Mary had tried both Viv and Sam, but neither had answered. Rose and Ruby were getting tired, and she had entertained them for long enough.

GiGi, ever the mother hen, offered her assistance. It was something they could all rely on. "Listen, Pops and I will be home in a jiffy, so just hang in there until we get home. I'll fix everything."

Poppy and GiGi had been worried about both their daughters. If it wasn't Mary's death-dreaming fiasco, it was Viv's dark mood. But in the midst of the turmoil, both of their girls had managed to remain responsible in caring for their homes and families. For Viv to not at least check in with her sister was odd and didn't settle well with GiGi or Poppy. GiGi dialed Viv several times in a row, but she didn't answer.

*****

About five miles outside of the area where the hunting cabin was hidden, Bonnie stopped the car and asked Viv to put on a blindfold and to allow her to tie her hands together with plastic zip ties.

"You're kidding, right?" Viv laughed.

She wasn't. After explaining that both Michael and Mary's lives would be in danger if she didn't cooperate, Viv agreed. Bonnie knew she would.

As they drove, Viv's mind was in a whirl. She wasn't necessarily afraid of Bonnie but definitely decided the blonde was certifiably insane. Curiosity is what caused her to agree to the blindfold and hand restraints. If Bonnie had any clues about Michael, Viv was all in.

When the car finally rolled to a stop, Bonnie promptly ran around the car to help Viv get out and stand to her feet. Bonnie, standing behind Viv with her hands on her shoulders, pushed her along. Viv's hands were bound and her eyes covered, but she intentionally tried to take in any clue that would give her a hint of where she'd been taken. She felt gravel beneath her feet and could hear no traffic sounds. They were definitely out in the boondocks. After taking three steps up, Viv heard a door swing open and felt a hard shove from behind. Falling forward a few strides, she managed to keep her balance and not hit the floor face first.

"Viv!", she heard.

The voice belonged to Michael.

*****

Once GiGi and Poppy got home from the church chili cook-off, they helped Mary get Rose and Ruby ready for bed. The sisters would be spending the night in Wills's room. Since the girls had been witnessing constant bickering from their parents, they were happy to have a peaceful change of pace.

GiGi, large and in charge, shoo'd Mary and Poppy out of the room so she could tell the girls a bedtime story. Even if it killed her, she was determined to make her mark and to be known as a favorite grandmother. After reading a quick book to them, she kissed their foreheads and tucked the covers beneath their bodies tightly. The two looked like little mummies.

"How did you do in the chili contest, GiGi?" Ruby asked. "Did you win?"

GiGi, unable to contain her malice, blurted out her opinion. "No, I didn't win. Aggie cheated. Can you believe that?"

"Cheated?" asked Rose, seemingly shocked. "Well, that's not right."

GiGi, taking this as an opportunity to teach a life lesson, sat down on the end of the bed to pontificate. "Girls, Aggie may have beat your old GiGi at that chili contest tonight, but cheaters never really win. There's such a thing as karma. Do y'all know what karma is?"

The fashionista Grandma who supported Gucci, Chanel, and Ralph Lauren as if they were part of her own family darted her eyes toward the girls. Her lipstick was still bright red on her lips and her eyeshadow applied perfectly. The girls were taking in all she had to say. Both shook their heads. They had no clue about karma.

"Karma is one of those wonderful things that God, in His goodness, created," she said, looking off into the distance as if capturing a slice of wisdom. "I guess you could call it a weapon that He uses to zap bad people who sin."

The girls turned their heads to look at one another. Their eyes grew wide as they considered all their own sins.

"When you do something bad to somebody," she said, "that same level of bad—plus a whole heck of a lot more—is gonna come right back atcha at lightning-bolt speed." As she spoke those last words, she slapped her hands loudly together.

The girls jumped.

"What does karma look like?" Rose asked. "Just so we'll know it when we see it?" In her mind, the girl with long black curls was picturing a large sword in God's hand, coming to slice away at the sinner. Coming to slice away at *her.*

"It's invisible," whispered GiGi, giggling and rubbing her palms together as she considered what was going to come to the one who'd cheated her out of the chili cook-off trophy. "And that's what makes it a perfect weapon, you see? When karma comes, the sinner never sees or hears it coming."

The girls' eyes were as big as saucers. This information was new to them. And it was horrifying.

"Always remember what the Good Book says," she added. "Your sins will surely find you out." Reaching for the light switch, she flicked it off, leaving the room pitch black. "No need to ever be a *karma chaser*, girls, because karma will always find who it's looking for on its own time."

And with that, GiGi left the room, feeling puffed up. She wouldn't lift a finger in vengeance; nor would she seek to repay evil with more evil. Aggie had karma coming to her and would pay for her sins soon enough.

*****

After scaring the girls half to death with her instruction about karma, GiGi adjourned to the kitchen. The old bird's voice had been soft as a pigeon with the girls, but she was ready to let the rest of the family know that her feathers were ruffled. "Where is that sorry-assed Sam?" she asked. "I'm just about ready to slap him with a frightful case of karma!"

Mary explained that Sam had told Viv he was working late, which is why she'd asked Mary to watch the girls. No one knew the name of the bride her sister was meeting or where they were meeting. As for Sam, he never answered his cell phone while working, so the fact that they couldn't reach him wasn't too worrisome. Just aggravating. But Viv? She would've called to check in.

GiGi, already flustered by her loss at the chili cook-off, became testier as each second passed. "OK, Mary," she began, "I know you think you're in some sort of death dream purgatory and that you believe none of this is actually happening...and I've been very patient with you as you've worked through your whackadoodle ways, wouldn't you agree?"

Mary, not sure where her mother was going with the tirade, rolled her eyes. "*I'm a whackadoodle*?" she asked, feeling particularly picked on. "Have you looked in a mirror?"

Mary's relationship with Philip appeared to be on an upswing, and as much as she wanted her life to be real, Mary reminded herself that this was still likely an alternate reality. There was a divine purpose for everything that was happening, and her job was to unlock the mystery. As such, she couldn't allow herself to be swayed off course no matter what her mother or anyone else said.

"Yes, honey bunch, you've been acting like you've got bats up in the belfry for far too long...and we've all been tip-toeing around you for fear you'll lose your mind and never find it again" GiGi said, her voice high pitched and shrill, "but it's high time for you to wake the hell up and snap out of this purgatory madness." Mary wanted to interrupt, to defend herself, but her mother was on a roll...not even taking a breath. "Your sister is down in the mouth with the depression, and now might be missing. Who knows? Maybe the sex traffickers have snatched her up." GiGi walked back and forth, using her hands for dramatic flair, as her imagination ran wild with the possibilities. "They might've lured Viv in, pretending to be a bride, for all we know. I've been told they look for Debbie Downers, and we all know your sister fits that bill as of late."

Mary couldn't help herself. She burst out in laughter. "Are you serious? Viv fits the sex-trafficking bill? Just how much would a man pay to have sex with a thirty-something-year-old woman who wears a doily on her head?" Just picturing it in her mind caused Mary to laugh all the more. "I'm pretty sure sex traffickers aren't interested in middle-aged cult women."

GiGi didn't appreciate the jab. She was trying to be patient with Mary and to reason with her, but all Mary could do was to make light of a very serious situation. Stomping her high heels on the kitchen floor, she shouted. "The point is, Mare Bear, I need you to come out of crazy town long enough to help me make sure your sister is alright. Can you do that? Between the two of you…and I can't believe I'm getting ready to say this…but you may be the one who is the *least* crazy. So I need you to buckle down and think of someone else besides yourself for a change."

"I'm not crazy," Mary said, feeling frustrated and worn down by everyone who couldn't see things the way she saw them. "Do you think I want to be dead?"

Mary rarely spoke of the mental gymnastics going on in her brain, and had never been quite so frank. "Gracious sakes, you're not dead. You've just been through so much trauma and under such stress that

your mind is working to find ways to protect itself."
GiGi felt for her daughter, but was still stern. Some-
thing had to give. "Do you live under a rock?
Haven't you ever heard of PTSD?"

"Can you prove I'm not dead?" asked Mary, setting
the stage to make a point. Putting her arms out,
she slowly spun around in a circle. "Can you prove
any of this is actually real and not a dream?"

GiGi, feeling as flustered as she'd ever felt in her
life, screamed. "Snap out of it this instant or you're
gonna end up losing Philip and your kids…I mean
it, you'll end up in a loony bin sucking apple sauce
up through a straw and hooked on old episodes of
The Golden Girls!"

Philip, who'd been busy trying to get Miss Charity to
sleep, walked into the room at the sound of all the
commotion. His presence completely threw GiGi.
Abashed and quite giddy about what appeared to
be a step forward in Mary's life, she chirped without
missing a beat. "Well, if it isn't Philip Montgomery,
standing strong alongside his family during their
time of need," she said, hoping he wouldn't realize
just how bonkers the mother of his children was for
fear he might bolt … and take the kids with him.

"Well hey there, GiGi…I thought I heard some good
redneck hurly-burly going on in here and had a feeling you were stirring things up." He walked over
and gave his former mother-in-law a big hug. She

sucked up the attention like a Hoover. "What did I miss?" he asked, his voice mellow and calm.

Philip was where he belonged. With Mary. GiGi, happy that at least one thing in her life was going right, turned to Mary. "What was it we were talking about, baby girl?" she asked, her mood now chipper and bright. "Let's fill Philip in while we have a cup of hot tea. Didn't you say you were making a pot of tea for your handsome ex-husband?"

Mary hadn't planned to make hot tea, but her mother's suggestion meant that she needed to begin boiling water. She'd do anything to keep her mother on some sort of happy note and off her back. Mary grabbed her tea kettle and began filling it with tap water while Philip opened the cabinet to retrieve four mugs.

"I think we were just about ready to talk about the chili cook-off," Mary said, hoping to switch the subject from Viv and herself for at least a half of a minute. "You never told me...did you win?" Mary's question brought GiGi crashing right back into reality.

*****

With the blindfold and plastic zip ties removed, Viv was chained to the bed just as Michael had been. It all seemed surreal to Viv, but she didn't fight. See-ing Michael was worth all the trauma and drama Bonnie could possibly unleash.

Bonnie forced Viv to address an envelope to Mary and write a letter explaining that she'd run away with Michael, that the two had been having a secret love affair, and that she was giving up her life to be with him. As Bonnie told her what to say, Viv wrote every word. It was true. Viv would gladly give up her life to be with Michael.

"All right, you naughty lovers, I'm going to go now and let you catch up," Bonnie said, grinning from ear to ear. "But don't do anything I wouldn't do," she added, laughing to herself as she turned out the light and left the room.

They were alone. Attached to the same bed. Viv grabbed Michael's face and kissed him, pressing her mouth against his so hard that it might bruise him. She didn't want to talk. Viv was back with her lover again.

Chapter 18

It had been a long evening. Not only had Preacher Walker and Jeannie been put in a predicament to manage the hullaballoo between GiGi and Aggie, but they'd also had to stay late to clean up the church after the chili cook-off. Tables and chairs had to be put away, floors had to be swept and mopped, and the kitchen counters needed wiped down. Being stewards of a church was not for the faint of heart.

When they finally hit the sack sometime after midnight, the last thing Jeannie wanted to think about was the chili cook-off. The sooner she could forget it, in fact, the better. As she worked on her nightly devotional, pen in hand, her husband laid on his back with his hands folded over his stomach. "What are we gonna do about GiGi and Aggie?" he asked, thinking back on the chili cook-off. "I'm afraid it's not gonna take long before those two gals go at it. I mean, fists and all."

The preacher and Jeannie had been married to each other for the majority of their lives, and what kept their union strong was their differences. As much as Jeannie wanted to forget the chili cook-off, Preacher Walker wanted to analyze it and find a solution. It was his way.

He wasn't confrontational, though. While Jeannie was willing to go head to head with just about anyone who was creating a disturbance in the church, he just wanted to pray about it. He was worrying about the situation, but she knew he wouldn't take any action at all.

"Listen, I don't want to waste my time thinking anymore about that chili cook-off because we both know you're not going to do a dad-blasted thing about it," she said, chuckling out loud. "Give me the go-ahead though, and I'll plan a meeting with the two of them right away. I'd be more than happy to set 'em straight."

She closed her Bible-study book, placed it on her nightstand, and folded her arms, knowing he'd never allow such a thing.

He shot her an apologetic smirk. She was right. "I'm sorry for disrupting your Bible study. It's just on my mind, that's all…and I reckon I wanna talk it out."

Jeannie knew him as well as she knew herself. He had the patience of Job and a dose of long-suffering to match it. But she worried. If GiGi and Aggie didn't find some kind of common ground soon, members would certainly find another church. People don't go to church to witness a brawl between two southern sinners who believe themselves to be saints. They needed to do something.

Preacher Walker burst out with an unexpected laugh as he thought of the two senior church ladies, dressed up in their finest Sunday attire, Bibles in hand, mouthing off at each other at every opportunity. His laughter caught Jeannie off guard.

"None of this is funny, you know," she said, snickering herself as she considered all the sass that fueled both GiGi and Aggie. "So what are we laughing about?"

"It's like a horribly written soap opera that no one wants to watch is playing out in our church," he replied, settling back down. "I guess we're all sinners who believe ourselves to be saints, though," he muttered, as if a nugget of truth had just plopped into his hand for safe keeping. "If I don't keep my guard up, I can get riled up from time to time at some of our deacons, you know. I'm just as big of a sinner as anybody."

Jeannie took a deep breath and then followed with a sigh. She loved the man. How could he possibly address two sinners when he saw himself as a sinner? "They're going to split the church if we're not careful," she said. Her voice was warm, not judgmental in the least. "All the church ladies are already taking sides."

It was true. GiGi and Aggie had strong personalities and were on opposing sides. The two were forces to be reckoned with.

"It's not my church, Jeannie," he said. The twinkle in his eye sparkled. "The church belongs to the Lord, and my calling is to preach the word to the best of my ability, to love and pray for the people, and to keep His house in tip-top condition."

How many times over the years had he said that same thing to her? She could've repeated the words if she'd wanted to but instead listened. She knew what his solution would be.

"Will ya pray with me about it?" he asked, turning his head toward her with eyebrows raised high and a half smile. "Where two or more are gathered," he added, reaching out his hand.

Jeannie shook her head and grinned. "I'll pray with you, Preacher, but I sure do wish you'd let me at 'em."

They shared another chuckle. The two were as different as night and day, but it worked. They prayed for the next several minutes that God would supernaturally intervene and bring the two families together. They both agreed reconciliation would have to begin with Mary and Philip.

"God, you're gonna have to work overtime on this one, I'm afraid," the old pastor prayed, still holding Jeannie's hand tight in his own. "And fair warnin', this may require a little extra creative power from above, because this family has more drama than Carter has peanuts…honest to goodness, Lord, I ain't never seen anything like it in my life."

An angel was nearby listening to the prayer that was offered in faith. Preacher Walker not only spoke the words but believed them in his heart. And as a result, his faith sent the angel to work.

Chapter 19

By the time the next morning rolled around, GiGi was in full-blown panic mode. Viv had never showed up or called. Something was up.

Sam had arrived at the old white house just before midnight, acting just as worried as the rest of the family. He'd shared an exchange of texts with Viv just before her scheduled meeting with the future bride where they discussed Rose and Ruby staying with Mary until she could pick them up. In the texts, he'd explained that he'd be working late. According to the story he told, he was making a run out of town to check pricing on potential fixtures for a bathroom remodel he was working on for some friends of theirs at church. It was all believable.

"But I haven't heard from her since," he told them, giving a commentary that clarified everything. A quick check on his outgoing calls showed he'd attempted to call her several times. "She never picked up," he said.

And of course, he knew they'd had the same experience.

Poppy contacted the police. GiGi put out a plea for any information concerning Viv's whereabouts on every social media outlet she could think of. And the family now sat down at the kitchen table to discuss how they'd explain all this to the children. How do you tell two little girls that their brand-new mom is missing?

"Sam, how much do you know about Rose and Ruby's birth mother?" GiGi asked, grasping at straws. "Is she the kind of person who'd be jealous and might harm Viv?"

Sam, careful to keep up the ruse, rubbed the long fuzz attached to his chin. "It's a possibility, I guess, but I can't really see it since the girls have been in foster care for a good bit."

It was true. If the girls' mother was going to get involved, it would've been before now. But there had to be a viable answer because Viv wasn't the type to run off.

It didn't take long for a call to come in verifying that Viv's car had been found at a sandwich shop just outside of town. But there was no sign of Viv and no one at the restaurant recalled seeing her there. Viv had vanished.

*****

When Wills finally awoke after another night of partying with friends, he checked his cell phone to find a text from his grandmother, Aggie. "Your Aunt Viv is missing. Just thought you'd want to know."

Pip and Aggie, who'd been absentee grandparents for most all his life, were now Wills's only connection to the rest of his family. His Aunt Viv had never been his favorite person in the world—her sarcastic humor wore thin at times—but regardless, he loved her. And he knew his GiGi and mother adored her.

He quickly shot Aggie a return text. "Thanks. Keep me posted." That was it. Wills was careful to not show any emotion. It was probably a protective mechanism.

Rolling over on his bed, he grabbed a spare pillow and pulled it tight to his chest. For a moment, he put his guard down. The news of Viv had gotten to him. His mind wandered to his sisters, Tate and Miss Charity. He wished he could call them and talk to them…or better yet, visit them. Viv's disappearance would rip the family's heart out. He knew they needed him.

Wills remained a college student, but only by the skin of his teeth. Balancing drugs, a party lifestyle, a part-time job, and a full school schedule was proving to be too much. Wills was imploding.

"Ask for help."

The voice in his head was so plain he couldn't ignore it.

"Go to your mom."

Again, the thought was as real as the pillow he held. But pride won out. Wills was determined that no one in his family would ever be put in a position of power or authority over him again. They'd kicked him out of their lives, and he would stay out. On his own.

*****

Together, Mary and GiGi conveyed the news about Viv to Tate, Rose, and Ruby, downplaying their concern as much as possible. Rose and Ruby were used to trauma, so they were more concerned about whether they'd be sent back into the foster-care system. The idea of home and family had always been just that to them…an idea, a dream, a happy ending that wasn't meant for them.

GiGi, noting their insecurity, pulled them both into her lap and assured them. "Girls, you are as much a part of this family as I am, which means you're not going anywhere." Planting a kiss on each of their cheeks, she continued. "Let's play a game. Can you tell me some facts you know about big, tall trees?"

The girls thought it was a rather odd time for a game, but GiGi always liked to play games, so they played along. Ruby answered first. "Well, a big giant tree has long branches and lots of leaves…you can hang a swing from it and swing really high too."

GiGi's eyes sparkled. "You're exactly right. Have you ever been on a swing that hangs from a tall tree?"

Ruby shook her head to indicate that she hadn't.

"Well then, Poppy will just have to hang a swing from one of the trees out in the yard. Maybe a tire swing!"

Ruby squealed with delight. "Yes, a tire swing! Pleeeaaaase!"

The proud grandmother smiled. Nothing made her nearly as happy as giving gifts to her grandchildren. "Rose, how about you, can you tell me what helps those tall trees to stand so tall?"

Rose answered quickly. "Roots."

"Oh my," bragged GiGi, "I knew you two were smart, but no one told me y'all were brilliant. Rose, you answered that so fast, and you are absolutely correct."

Rose was pleased. "I know lots of stuff," she added.

"I'm sure you do," GiGi said, nodding her head with approval. "But I've got a tougher question for you to consider. Are you ready?"

"Of course I'm ready," answered Rose.

"OK, here goes. Without the roots, what would happen to those tall trees?"

"They'd fall down flat," answered Rose.

"Timberrrrr!" added Ruby, giggling.

"Exactly. And ever since your adoption, this family has become your roots," GiGi proclaimed, exuding confidence and pride. "You girls are going to grow up into tall, beautiful, healthy trees while the rest of us hold you up, support you, and give you nourishment." The girls were listening intently to their grandmother. She had their full attention.

"Where do the roots grow, Ruby?" GiGi asked, singling out the youngest of the two.

"Under the ground where you can't see them," said the little girl, her eyes filled with innocence, even though she'd had a tattered past that had robbed her from so much.

"Correct again. And the reason they're under the ground is so no one can touch them or bother them…so no matter what, that tree is safe. In that exact same way, you're both safe. Just think of me up under the ground holding you up." GiGi hugged them tight. They allowed themselves to melt into her arms.

"How easy is it to pick a great big tree up and move it?" Poppy asked. He was sitting nearby listening to the conversation.

Simultaneously, they both replied, a silly sneer shining forth from both of their faces. "You can't pick up a tree, Pops!"

"That's right, girls. A tree is planted firmly into the ground. It's not going anywhere. And you're not going anywhere either." Poppy walked over and joined in on all the hugging.

The foursome hugged one another tight. Ruby nestled her nose into GiGi's neck. She felt safe with her.

"All righty, Pops," Gigi announced, "why don't you go fetch us girls a few Oreo cookies from the pantry? You know how much young ladies need chocolate to keep 'em trucking along." GiGi raised an arm and pretended to be a trucker pulling down on her truck's horn. "Toot! Toot!" she shouted.

The girls clapped their hands with glee. They loved their new grandmother more than they could express. She was their favorite person in the world, just what they'd always wished for.

Poppy was happy to oblige. His heart was heavy with worry for his daughter, Viv, but it was equally heavy for Rose and Ruby. He wondered what was happening to his family. If a cookie would help, he was going to provide as many as their tummies could hold.

As Poppy was busy opening the pantry and pulling out a box of Oreo cookies, GiGi expounded upon the thoughts that were running rampant in her heart. "Let your roots grow deep so you can stand tall, you hear?" she whispered. "You girls are going to be the envy of the forest…two giant oak trees among straggly, sappy pines." She kissed each on the forehead. "You just spread your branches as wide as they'll go while reaching up toward the Son of God. He's the light that will nourish you, while I'm your biggest root of all. We won't let you down. Ever. I promise."

*****

Wills, sick of feeling anything at all, rose from his bed to find a little orange pill. Within minutes of popping the meds and chasing with alcohol, he'd be feeling energized and in control again. He deserved that much.

But just as his feet hit the floor, he remembered he'd run out. He'd passed a couple out to friends and intended to refill his stash but hadn't gotten around to it. Slamming the wall with his hand, he let out a loud grunt.

"Wills, man, what the hell is wrong with you?" yelled one of his roommates from another room. He opened the door and walked in. "Are you all right?"

"No, I'm not all right," answered Wills, scratching the top of his head. "I'm out of Adderall, dude, which means I need you to set me up with the supplier right away."

His roommate was happy to supply Wills with all that he needed since he got a cut of every sale. "I'll call him now, but while you wait, I've got some Vicodin."

Vicodin. It was an opiate. Hydrocodone. Pain pills. Scratch. Vikes. And Wills had avoided opiates for fear of becoming even more addicted. Heroin is an opiate, and he had plenty of friends who were miserably strung out and dependent. Most of them had started out with Vicodin.

"Nah, I'll wait on the Adderall," he responded, certain he could wait for what had become his drug of choice. Pulling a bottle of vodka from his dresser drawer, he downed two shots as if it were water. "I'm already pretty addicted to Adderall and don't think I need another pill addiction." He laughed. Addicted. He'd said the word out loud.

His roommate saw the weakness. Wills wreaked of it. Leaving the room, he pretended to make a call to his supplier. Wills strained his ears to hear his roommate's side of the conversation. "You can't get the pills to us for a couple of days? Really?...OK, I'll tell Wills...Yeah, I'm pretty sure he can hold out until then. Thanks."

Wills, unable to hold back his feelings, tore out of his room and confronted his roommate. "I can't wait for a couple of days, man! Don't you have another supplier?" He was breaking out into a cold sweat.

His roommate feigned concern. "I wish I did...but nah, things don't work that way. Like I said before, I've got that Vicodin. Just say the word, and it's yours."

Chapter 20

It was when Philip brought in the mail that every-thing in GiGi, Poppy, and Mary's world shifted yet again. GiGi held the opened letter in her hands and recognized the handwriting immediately. It was from Viv.

Clearing her throat with a sudden obtrusive cough, she made a request. "Tater Bug, I need you to take the girls to Miss Charity's room for just a few min-utes while I talk to the adults about boring adult stuff, all right?" The matriarch's joyful demeanor be-lied all she felt inside. In truth, her head was spin-ning and her stomach churning.

Tate gave her grandmother a sideways glance. GiGi read her granddaughter's thoughts loud and clear. "Don't worry, we're just gonna discuss busi-ness that has to do with some bills that need to be paid. I assure you, you wouldn't be interested in the least." Deciding she really wasn't interested in adult talk, Tate motioned for her sister and young cousins to follow her. And one by one, they traipsed off to-gether, clueless.

GiGi lowered her voice and raised her eyebrows: "As for the rest of you, follow me to the master bed-room. What I'm about to announce is going to re-quire complete privacy from those girls and I'm not entirely sure they won't be sneaky with their little ears."

Turning her heels, the mother hen marched toward the bedroom, motioning for the group to follow her. And just as the young girls had followed Tate to Miss Charity's bedroom, Poppy, Mary, Philip, and Sam followed right behind the feisty grandma. Once everyone was in Mary's bedroom, GiGi locked the door and turned on the TV for noise that would cover up what she had to tell them.

"You've got to be kidding me, Momma," said Mary, rolling her eyes. "This is overkill even for you."

Gripping the letter between her fingers, she shook it at Mary. "Overkill?" she asked, her face twisted with disgust. "This letter happens to be from your no-good, sorry, cheating sister!"

*****

Michael and Viv had spent the night catching up in all sorts of ways, most involving barely clothed bodies and extreme passion. She hadn't felt frightened at all. She'd rather die with Michael than live without him.

Bonnie had returned to the cabin at some point during the night. They'd heard her drive up, followed by the cabin door opening and closing. She'd breezed into their room for a brief moment that morning, not saying anything, but giving them their rationed food portions for the day.

"Bonnie and Sam are nuts," Michael said once he knew they were once again alone in the cabin. "We've gotta figure out how to get out of here because they really are planning to kill us."

Viv hadn't seen Sam yet, but Michael had filled her in on everything. She was sure it wouldn't be long before he showed up, and she dreaded what he might do to her.

"You're right. Bonnie is off-the-charts mentally insane, and I have no idea what Sam has said or done to pull her into this crazy crime zone with him." She took a deep breath before continuing; it was all so much to take in. "Sam is driven by his far-out religious beliefs…and I would know about how powerful those beliefs are because I was almost taken in by it." Viv spoke freely with Michael, describing the time she spent in the cult and Sam's constant lordship over her. "He follows the Old Testament of the Bible and believes he has the right to control my life, to destroy my life, and I guess to take my life."

"Well he's not married to me, so what Old Testament scripture gives him authority over my life?" Michael's question seemed reasonable enough.

"You had sex with his wife," Viv answered. "That's adultery. And so in Sam's mind, we both are deserving of death."

Looking into Michael's eyes, she brushed his hair back from his face and softly recited Leviticus 20:10, a verse Sam had used to torment her many times: "And the man that committeth adultery with another man's wife, even he that committeth adultery with his neighbor's wife, the adulterer and the adulteress shall surely be put to death."

Michael blinked hard. "Oh my God, we've got to get out of here."

*****

"You better take a seat over there on the side of the bed, Sam." GiGi pointed to the bed with one hand and gave Sam a shove with the other. "And after this, I may need a stiff drink or two." She didn't drink. Anyone who knew her knew alcohol had never touched her lips and never would.

"Lord have mercy, Momma, would you please cut the drama and just tell us what the letter says?" Mary's concern for her sister was obvious. She didn't have time for her mother's shenanigans. "Unless Viv has been kidnapped and the kidnappers are demanding a big ransom, you need to just lay it on us already."

With Sam seated on the bed and the rest of the group standing awkwardly around the room, waiting for her to expound upon what she'd read in Viv's letter, GiGi began. "This is way worse than Viv being kidnapped, honey bunch...I guarantee you that."

Mary was a skeptic. Her sister was as dependable as the tick of a clock. Now part of Sam's cult, her skirts hung at her ankles and a doily covered her head. Viv was reliable, a rule follower, and boring.

"Like I said before, it turns out Viv is a cheater," GiGi said, shaking her head, "and I'm sorry about that, Sam, because quite honestly I've been secretly thinking you're nothing more than a scum bag. But it's my own daughter...my own flesh and blood...who appears to be the scum."

Before Mary could say anything, Sam spoke up. "A cheater? What are you saying? Viv cheated on me?" Sam's questions were expertly delivered. He was a husband scorned. Aghast. Shocked. Hurt. "Who's the bastard? I'll kill him."

*****

Michael and Viv spent the next couple of hours trying to figure out how to free themselves without any luck. Both were chained to the bed with keyed disc padlocks. The bed had been masterfully bolted to the wall and floor. "To free ourselves would require that we tear part of the wall down and drag parts of the floor out with us as well," Michael explained, frustrated beyond belief. He'd been trying to figure out an escape for weeks, but with Viv by his side, he felt even more determined to be free. "I think it's impossible."

Viv was in full agreement. Breaking free was an impossibility, but she had another idea. "What if we could get Bonnie to set us free?" she asked.

Michael, who'd been spending a lot of time with Bonnie, huffed. "She's a psycho, Viv. Bonnie's been drinking Sam's Kool-Aid. I don't think there's much hope there."

Viv loved him. She had to be with him for the rest of her life. And if that meant manipulating Bonnie Cutless, she was up for the challenge. "Not much hope sounds pretty darned good when compared to no hope at all." Tilting her head to the right, she grinned and leaned in to plant a soft kiss on Michael's mouth. Yes, she was chained to a bed and being threatened with certain murder, but she was with Michael. Her life ironically felt more right than it had in a very long time.

Chapter 21

The group had stuck together the entire evening and were up into the wee hours of the morning trying to come up with answers. Finally, they all agreed to try to get some sleep, but they didn't rest much at all. How could they? Viv was gone, and they were reeling with worry.

Even Sam and Philip had slept over at the old white house. Rose and Ruby crashed in the floor of Tate's room, Philip took Wills's room, and Sam was relegated to the sofa. In GiGi's mind, the bearded cult man wouldn't be a part of their family much longer, so his comfort was at the bottom of her list.

In spite of the apprehensive mood in the house, the following morning Sam announced he was leaving his girls at the old white house to go search for Viv and Michael. He announced without any misgiving that he didn't know when he'd return, but that when he did return, Viv would be with him.

"I'm sure Viv was just feeling overwhelmed with life, considering the adoption and all, and I bet Michael swooped in offering her promises of a simpler life," he told them. "This is a midlife crisis at best...or it could even be a full mental breakdown." His act of concern seemed genuine.

GiGi, Poppy, and Mary were feeling so bone-weary and devastated that it actually seemed reasonable for Sam to leave Rose and Ruby behind to search for his wife. Mary did bring up the possibility that a kidnapper could've forced Viv to write the letter, while GiGi bantered about the notion that a sex trafficker might've taken her, but Sam had an answer for that too.

"You know, Viv never fully bonded with those girls, and she felt guilty about it," he told them, developing his story. "So, if Michael came calling on her, it would make sense that he'd be a way for her to escape those feelings."

And that too sounded rational. How many times had Viv complained about the girls' bad behavior? The decision to adopt them had come from the pressure she felt to become pregnant. Looking back, the pieces seemed to fit together. Maybe Viv did run off with Michael.

The family wished Sam good luck, asked him to check in with them once a day to give an update, and even hugged him when he left. He mentioned he was hiring a private investigator to help him find clues. He appeared on top of things and eager to find his wife. "Don't worry," he added before leaving. "I've already forgiven my wife, and we will be a family again." The man deserved an Oscar.

Miss Charity was the first of the children to awake, and with eyes wide open, she was ready to tackle the day. Unable to comprehend the impending drama taking place with her family, the little girl with ringlet curls simply wanted to play. Mary, in a stupor from lack of sleep, opened the back door to allow her to go outside while she fixed a pot of coffee. Trudy, the little girl's faithful companion, scooted off right behind her.

Digging in the dirt was Miss Charity's plan for the day, so she quickly got to work. Expeditiously scraping her fingernails against the cool gritty earth, she skillfully dislodged the soil from its resting place. Seated with her rump on the ground, before long, she'd gathered enough dirt to blanket her legs and bare feet. Every few minutes, she'd rub the dirt into her skin and onto her hair and face, never taking the time to consider why she enjoyed it so much. Trudy, taking Miss Charity's lead, instinctively dug right along beside her. This was one of their favorite things to do together. It was a good day.

Both were so busy digging into the ground that they didn't notice when Bonnie Cutless slipped in through the back gate. In fact, it wasn't until she was right up on them that they spotted her. Miss Charity, immediately recognizing Bonnie, jumped up to offer a big hug.

"No, no, no," Bonnie said, backing away and grimacing at the thought of being touched by such dirty hands. Kneeling down to the small dog, who was wagging her tail with joy at seeing a familiar face, Bonnie lowered her voice and mumbled something about feeling bad about what she was about to do.

Hanging from her hand was a cold steel knife with a jagged blade. She pulled Trudy's neck back at a hard angle and sliced it open with great force.

Miss Charity stood before the woman, head tilted and with a half grin on her face. Was this a new game?

The one who knew no evil couldn't possibly wrap her mind around the depravity and maliciousness she'd just witnessed. There had to be another explanation. Death in such a brutal fashion was beyond her grasp.

Standing over the convulsing body of the family's pet, Bonnie snapped a picture with her cell phone. Sam wanted proof.

"This is your momma's fault," was all Bonnie said as she turned to leave. The wicked deed was done in less than five minutes of time.

As the gentle breeze blew through the property's trees, life drifted from the dog's body. The little girl, confused by the blood and not understanding why Trudy had stopped playing with her, crumpled herself upon the ground next to her best friend. Something was very wrong. Miss Charity's angel, true to form and ever faithful, laid by her side on the hard earth, hugging her close. He'd known this was coming and had been dreading it.

The two lay next to Trudy for more than half an hour, when Mary finally came out to check on her daughter. Standing in the open doorway, she called, "It's time for breakfast! Come in you two!"

Miss Charity and Trudy were an inseparable duo. Ever since Wills had left the picture, the youngest Montgomery had grown even closer to her furry friend. GiGi often remarked that Trudy had sensed Miss Charity's pain in losing her big brother and had stepped up to the plate. Yes, Wills was very much alive, but his absence felt very much like a death to the entire family. The grief was eerily similar.

When Miss Charity didn't come to the door, Mary stepped out onto the back porch. "Miss Charity, did you hear me? It's time to come in!"

By this time, everyone was beginning to gather around the kitchen table. GiGi had thrown together a breakfast casserole the night before and it was reheating in the oven. A bowl of fresh fruit and a pitcher of orange juice would complete the small feast. The adults were already discussing their plans for trying to locate Viv, so Mary, hearing their conversations, became distracted and moved back inside.

It was when everyone was seated, prepared to eat, that she thought of Miss Charity again. The back-door had remained open, but the girl hadn't come in. As it is with moms of kids who have special needs, panic suddenly struck her like an electric shock. Jumping up from the table like she'd been shot, Mary darted out the door. "Miss Charity! Where are you?" she shouted, running into the yard like a woman who'd lost her mind.

GiGi and Philip, more concerned about Mary than Miss Charity, rose from the table and stood at the open doorway. "God, she's nuts," GiGi chirped. "Both of my daughters are just plain nuts."

Philip put his arm around his mother-in-law's shoulder. He knew how Mary's mental state had worn on the woman, and now with Viv's disappearance, he wondered how her own state of mind would fare. GiGi was strong, but she was getting older.

"I guess you think I'm nuts too, don't you?" she asked, patting the hand that was placed on her shoulder. "Lord, I'd have to be nuts to put up with all of you." A slight grin crept up on her unexpectedly. Her daughter, Viv, was missing. This was no time for joking.

Philip didn't hesitate with his own smile. "You're the best kind of nuts," he answered, pulling her in closer to him. His heart hurt for the woman who'd been there for his family throughout the years, the one who never gave up on Mary and him.

In response, GiGi allowed herself to laugh. He'd put her through hell and back with the Bonnie Cutless saga and the penis photo that had made its way around town courtesy of the worldwide web, but she loved Philip. He'd been a part of her life since he was just a boy.

At the same time, Mary had spotted Miss Charity. When she saw her little girl and Trudy laying on the ground, covered in dirt and blood, her first thought was that they were both dead. And something within her snapped. She felt it. Then a sound came out of her mouth that she had no control over. It was a throaty screech. And with the sound, GiGi and Philip jumped as the hair on their bodies stood on end.

Chapter 22

The cabin was dark and dank but desperately held onto a slight scent of cedar from its lined closets. Viv wondered how long Sam had owned the cabin and how often during their brief marriage he'd visited it. From the looks of the place, he'd probably built it himself over a long period of time. A single man with wood-working skills is capable of such things.

There was a main room, set off with a green plaid couch and matching recliner. Both looked like they'd clawed and scraped their way out of the seventies, but they were clean and looked fairly new. A small kitchen bar lined with a couple of homemade wooden stools separated the room, and on each side of the space was a bedroom large enough to house a full-sized bed. Michael estimated the place to be less than eight hundred square feet in size. It had been built for pragmatic purposes only.

Off the grid, what little power the cabin could muster was a gift from the sun by way of a few solar panels, a backup generator, and propane. Knowing Sam, he'd probably bartered for most of it. The composting toilets were small but functional for the purpose they served, and the area's natural springs made the cabin a perfect spot for the well that pumped water onto the property. Sam's hideaway cabin was a perfect self-sustaining prison.

When Sam strutted into the cabin with his hand around Bonnie's waist, Viv lost all feeling in her arms and legs. She'd been held captive for two days and now would be forced to face the monster who was behind the terrorizing theatrics. Taking a deep breath, she prepared to be the target of her husband's pent-up fury. Michael had coached her on how to shut her mind down and to not listen to what Sam had to say, so Viv carefully stiffened her body, cleared her mind, and braced herself for Sam's vitriol. No matter what happened, she would not engage the man in a war of words. Michael had instructed her to behave as a subdued prisoner, and she would do so for their safety.

Ironically, though, Sam didn't speak a word or even look Viv's way. As soon as he and Bonnie entered the cabin, the duo went into the adjacent bedroom and closed the door. Viv should've felt a sense of calm, considering she'd avoided a clash the size of the first battle of Bull Run, but in reality, she felt a craving for blood. She was ready to kill the man who'd become the bane of her existence.

"Sam!" she hollered, her voice booming through the small wooden cabin.

Michael, startled by her sudden outburst, shushed her. "Viv, don't engage him," he reminded her. But her focus was on the spouse she'd pledged her life to. Her abuser. Her kidnapper.

"Sam, you demon from hell," she yelled, with the full breadth and capacity her lungs would allow, "come out here and face me!"

No answer. No response.

Michael, growing more uneasy, pleaded with her to let it go. He reminded her that Sam's actions had nothing to do with her, that he was mentally ill, and that to rile him up would likely do more harm than good. "God, Viv, if you keep screaming like this, Sam might come out here and shoot us right now," he urged.

Viv looked down at her wrist. It was already turning blue from the chain that bound her. She then looked into the crystal blue pools of Michael's eyes. He was the man who was meant to be her husband, the one she loved more than air, and the man Sam was planning to kill. As much as the five fingers on each of her hands were motivated to reach out to gently touch the face of her lover, hate was the current emotion driving her to picture using those same hands to choke the life out of Sam.

"You're nothing but a coward, Sam Smith!" she screamed, her face burning with fury. "And if I'm going to bust hell wide open for having a love affair with Michael, just know that you won't be too far behind me. Murder is a sin, you fool!"

Her breathing was erratic as she fought crossing over into a mental state she'd never return from.

"Read the Ten Commandments, Sam! Murder is a sin! A big one!" Tears sprang from her eyes as hysteria set in. "Do you hear me, Sam Smith? You'll go straight to hell if you murder us!"

Viv knew the remaining time she had with Michael was limited. They were both as good as dead. Michael knew it too. He reached out his arms and pulled her tightly into him. "I love you, Michael," she sobbed, her voice breaking violently as she gave up the fight. "I'm so sorry I brought you into this."

Sam, in the next room, smirked. His white teeth shined through his burly beard, displaying all he felt inside. He'd heard every venomous word shouted by Viv but chose not to bite on what she was serving. He didn't need to because Viv and Michael were suffering. They were his prisoners. And while he was now in charge of every breath they took, he'd soon be in charge of their heinous deaths.

Bonnie watched Sam closely. Through the years, she'd been involved with many men who were very much like him. They'd forced themselves upon her when she was just a young teenager, caught up in an occult that believed in sex-sharing. "You live for this, don't you?" she asked, feeling suddenly turned on by the man who was successfully conquering those who'd beguiled him. Falling back onto the bed, she raised her arms above her head and twisted into a pin-up pose. Wearing tight leggings, pumps, and a fitted short-sleeved pale pink sweater, the pose served her well.

Sam took a seat opposite her on a wooden stool and rested his elbows on his knees. "Do you want to know what I live for?" he asked, realizing Bonnie was now in his grasp. "I live for love, baby," he said, reaching up to tug on his beard. "The Lord created us for love, Bonnie."

Bonnie knew where this was going. It was now a freight train that couldn't be stopped.

"But God didn't create your awful beard, Sam," she laughed, rolling her eyes. "And I'm not sure I could make love with you unless you'd be willing to let me clip your straggly hair and trim the fuzz from your rugged, handsome face." She was toying with him, and he liked it. "I think we could cook up some really outstanding love," she said, seductively luring him in, "don't you?" Pushing herself up to one elbow, Bonnie allowed her eyes to fix upon his. "Wouldn't you like to fool around with me, Sam?"

His body quickly told him the answer. It was a resounding yes.

*****

GiGi may have been decades older than Philip, but she was the first to get to Mary, Miss Charity, and their beloved dog in the backyard that day. Without hesitation, she took off in a shot at the sound of her daughter's scream. It's what mommas do.

As the heart of her family, it was GiGi's job to keep everything together. She'd always been stalwart in her purpose. For her, family always came first. But when she saw Miss Charity and Trudy lying on the ground together, covered in dirt and blood, she grabbed hold of Mary's arm to steady herself and froze. At once, her mind melted away into a dark chasm of obscurity as she stood at her daughter's side, staring at the horrible sight. It was too much to bear. In that moment, GiGi needed help too.

When Philip arrived, only seconds behind GiGi, he impulsively fell to his knees and scooped Miss Charity up into his arms. Because of the girl's low muscle tone, Miss Charity's body fell like a rag doll. Like GiGi and Mary, Philip too thought she'd passed. "No, this can't be happening," he said, kissing her forehead while rocking back and forth. Placing his ear to her mouth, he carefully listened for a breath. GiGi and Mary stood close by, still unable to respond; they were clearly in shock. Philip turned toward them, tears streaming down his face. "Mary," he cried, "oh my God, this can't be happening."

Philip's words snapped Mary out of her stupor. She fell to her knees beside Philip. If they were going to go through this horror, they would do it together.

Miss Charity, the little girl with no words, lifted her hand to touch her daddy's cheek. When his eyes met hers, she smiled at him with the purest of innocence. Elation and relief swept over Philip like a wave that sneaks up out of nowhere and knocks you down deep into the depths of the ocean. Gasping to find air, the man who'd been in her life since the moment she took her first breath whimpered, "You're alive! Praise the Lord, you're alive!"

Sensing her daddy's emotions, the little one pulled herself up and wrapped her arms around his neck. Philip nuzzled his face into the crook of her neck. "Thank you, God," he muttered through great emotion, unable to find his full voice.

Mary planted her face into her hands and wept tears of great relief. GiGi, still standing at their backs, passed out cold.

Chapter 23

When Sam entered Viv and Michael's room with a clean-shaven face and modern haircut, Viv just about croaked. Bonnie, scandalously dressed in a short silky robe, sauntered in close behind him, holding his hand. The two didn't attempt to hide the newfound closeness between them.

Sam was the first to speak. "Because of your sin," he announced, referring to both Michael and Viv, "I've now sinned." The man was rattled; there was no mistake about it. And Sam being rattled didn't necessarily bode well for the prisoners, so Michael immediately began to think of how he could turn the tide. For the moment, though, he'd be all ears.

"Since my sexual needs were not being met by my wife, I committed adultery with this woman." Sam nodded his head toward Bonnie as he spoke. In response, Bonnie blew him a kiss.

"Do you see?" he continued, now singling Viv out with the brunt of his stare. "Sin perpetuates sin, so you and Michael must pay the ultimate price very soon before the sex continues to escalate out of control."

"That's right," interjected Bonnie, "because I can see a hell of a lot of sex in our future." She straightened her robe and pushed her hair back from her face. "My sexual needs haven't been met as of late either."

Was she making a joke or was the blond tramp serious? No one really knew. And Michael noticed Viv's face was getting redder by the minute.

Sam, overly theatrical and painfully hokey, threw his head back and closed his eyes. "She's right. Sin has an awful pull. It's why David fell for Bathsheba and ended up having her husband killed on the battlefield. But God forgave David." Pulling his head back down, he folded his hands up under his chin. "Thank you, God, for the gift of forgiveness," he prayed, mostly for show.

Viv and Michael, who'd been aware of Sam sleeping over in the cabin, had already discussed how they'd use this new piece of information to benefit their cause. Forget David and Bathsheba, it was more like Sampson had fallen prey to Delilah in that cabin, which meant Sam had shown a sign of weakness. Not only had he had sex with Bonnie, but he'd allowed her to shave his hair and beard. It was a sign from God, and they needed to make every attempt to use it to their advantage. Hadn't Delilah been the impetus to Sampson's demise? First and foremost, however, they had to keep Sam calm.

Viv tired to shove her pent up anger and disgust down deep into her belly. It was like swallowing bitter bile that comes up into your throat with a bad case of indigestion. "Sam, I agree. Your sin is on Michael and me." She nearly choked on the lie. Getting the hollow words out was more difficult than she anticipated, so she paused briefly and pretended to feel remorse. "It's our fault for having the affair in the first place," she said, blurting the words out as fast as she could, before losing her stick-to-itiveness.

As she spoke, Michael nodded his head in agreement. Viv felt a sudden itch and scratched her neck. She was breaking out in hives. This ruse was going to be hard to keep up.

Sam, feeling a sermon rising up inside of him, paced back and forth in the small bedroom. "I loved you, Viv," he began, acting as if he'd been jilted in the worst possible way. "You know, I honestly believed the good Lord brought us together in marriage for life...but you went and questioned my religion, and in doing so, you questioned my God and my manhood. You're the reason I started hitting you. It's time for you to admit this is all your fault. You screwed everything up."

Viv wanted to do what Michael had asked her to do. She wanted to appear authentic, contrite, and humble. Their lives depended on it. But the woman was thrown. "I'm sorry, but I feel like I'm on the Jerry Springer Show," she muttered, wanting desperately to wipe the smug look off of Sam's face with the flat end of a shovel. She'd never seen her husband without a beard. He looked like a completely different person. And Sam was insane to blame her for his abuse. The bumps on her neck started to spread down to her chest. At this point, she was rubbing and scratching like a dog with fleas. Sam noted her preoccupation.

"Viv, if you've got something to say to me, speak up loud and clear," he said. "It's your life that's at stake here, you know. I'd just as soon shoot you as look at you."

Michael, determined to pull the conversation back around, interrupted. "Sam, if I could just interject here…I think what you're forgetting is where scripture says that all of us have sinned and have fallen short of the glory of God. No matter how perfect we try to be, and I'm sure you've worked really hard at being the best person you can be, none of us will ever hit the mark because we're human." He shot Viv a quick wink of his eye, encouraging her to stick with their plan. "You're a human, Sam, just like Viv and me. We've all made mistakes here."

Michael was doing his best to assuage Sam of any guilt, to make him feel a connection with him.

"Well, in the Bible," Sam said, still pacing the floor and still hoping to feel better about his night in the sack with Bonnie, "King Solomon had hundreds of wives and must've had sex with them all. What got him was that he started worshipping the idols instead of God. It wasn't the sex that got him, it was the idols." His southern drawl was as thick as butter, and he slathered it on particularly heavy when speaking of religious matters.

Viv couldn't believe her ears. Sam was actually going to rationalize adultery. Was he really that big of an idiot? Solomon's sexual desire for the women who were worshipping idols is what caused him to cross spiritual boundaries. But she had to stay silent. Her job was to keep Sam calm.

"I've never worshipped idols of any sort," Sam said, "and I've only had sex with the two women in this room…and one was a lot more enjoyable than the other."

Was he actually going to compare them?

Bonnie raised her hand and waved it around. "Me!" she shouted, as if giving a victory cheer, "I'm the one who's more enjoyable."

Viv couldn't believe it. This was worse than a Jerry Springer Show … it was a full-blown circus. And Sam and Viv were the stars of the freak parade.

Sam stopped mid-stride and looked directly at both Michael and Viv. "Even without my beard, I still love the Lord with all my heart. I think I just fell in a moment of weakness to a temptress."

Bonnie giggled. She liked being called a temptress. At the sound of her laugh, Sam turned toward her and sighed. She'd been worth the fall. "Not to mention," he said, pointing at Bonnie, "having sex outside of my marriage with that woman is a result of the two of you hopping in the sack together. You started it, so the sin is really heaped upon you two."

The bountiful blonde blew Sam another kiss. He pretended to catch it in his hand and then moved over close to face Bonnie. Viv slapped her free hand onto her face so hard, the sound caused Michael to wince. But he understood. The entire state of affairs was over the top. Viv was chained to a bed with her lover while her abusive husband and his new lover were devising a plan to murder them. And as if that wasn't enough, Sam and Bonnie were justifying it all using the Bible.

"As soon as we lure Mary here into this cabin," Sam said, grinning from ear to ear as he took Bonnie's hands into his, "this mess will all be behind us and we can move on with our new life together." The cult man's mood shift was so light-hearted and sunny, if he'd been soil, he might've sprouted a flower on the spot. Viv's body, in response to his sappy harangue, became one big hive.

"You're the woman I'm meant to be with, Bonnie," he continued, "and God will bless our union with a child. Even now you may be with child. I truly believe it." Sam dropped Bonnie's hands and grabbed her waist. Pulling her tight into him, he kissed her passionately.

At that point, Viv couldn't hold back. "I don't even care about you and Bonnie having a love child. Lord have mercy, you don't know how much I don't care." The words rushed out of her mouth like a bunch of firemen running toward a burning building, desiring to reach out and extinguish the filthy fire they were aiming for. "But you've got Michael and me," she yelled, panic cutting off each word sharply as she breathed heavily, "so why do you need to lure Mary here to this snake pit of a cabin?"

Sam ignored her and continued to kiss Bonnie, allowing his hands to work their way all over her body without caution. He wanted Viv to see and hoped that his physical actions with Bonnie would sting. Bonnie played right along with the game, openly accepting all Sam had to give.

Viv clenched her fists, allowing her nails to dig deep into the palms of her hands. She didn't care near as much about her own safety as she did for the safety of her sister. Mary had been through so much already. Viv could *not* allow her marriage to a nutcase to impact the rest of her family. "Answer me, dammit!" she screamed, completely out of control. "What does Mary have to do with any of this, Sam?"

Bonnie pulled away from Sam. While *he* didn't plan to dignify his wife with any sort of response, Bonnie was eager to cram her plans down Viv's throat. Setting her jaw and narrowing her eyes, she looked right into Viv's eyes. "Are you a complete imbecile?" she asked, speaking to Viv as if she were nothing more than an aggravating flea. "You and Michael are fodder for Sam…but Mary, my dear, is for me."

Reality hit Viv like a brick in the face. "Oh God," she gasped, now seeing the plan clearly. Michael took her hand and held it tight.

Not only were she and Michael going to die, but Mary was going to die also.

Chapter 24

The only way Mary could function was to keep herself safely tucked inside her death-dream bubble. Nothing else made sense. Her family had tried to convince the police that the dog's massacre in the backyard was somehow connected to Viv's sudden disappearance, but the officers insisted Viv's letter proved she'd run away with her lover. They'd also said that while abandoning her children *did* demonstrate that Viv wasn't a very good parent, the information was not worthy of launching a missing person's search.

"How about our dog, Trudy?" Mary had asked them. "Maybe my family is being targeted by someone who's deranged. Will they kill one of us next? What if they've already kidnapped or murdered Viv?"

She asked question after question without taking a breath, and the police officers were polite and listened to every question she asked. They explained, however, that there had been other pets who'd been killed the same way. "I know it's hard to grasp," they'd said, "but things like this happen sometimes with gang initiations or with troubled teenage kids who are hoping to draw attention to themselves. Teens sometimes do outlandish things like this so they can see their crimes mentioned in the news."

It was sick. Mary's mind couldn't comprehend it. This was her perfectly southern hometown, where there was a church on every corner. The city embraced Jesus at Christmas and Easter and held prayer vigils for people who were in need. The local businesses offered shelter for the homeless and provided food pantries for the hungry. When a funeral procession drove by, everyone in town stopped to honor the dead. And almost every home raised a flag on the Fourth of July. How could this be?

The police had thought this through and were being reasonable. Mary knew it. Why alarm an entire city of people when it was a possibility, even though highly unlikely in her mind, that Trudy was killed by a group of teenagers who'd taken crime to the next level and that her sister had run off with her first love? One thing was certain, however. Mary's heart was hurting like never before. Not only was Viv gone, but her dog had been killed.

Miss Charity had an unresolved heart issue and remained non-verbal. Wills had estranged himself from the family. Philip almost married another woman. Trudy was now dead. Mary was living in the old white house that was now owned by her parents. And Viv had taken off with Michael. No matter how Mary tried to accept things, nothing added up. The family had always sought to live lives that pleased God, and they'd been decent citizens, neighbors, and friends. What had they done to deserve all the upheaval?

Mary's mind settled upon her sister. Viv appeared to have a healthy marriage to Sam. Hadn't she just adopted two little girls with the man? Mary knew her sister better than anyone else. Viv would never walk away from responsibilities and commitments. To her knowledge, prior to her sister's involvement with Sam and the cult, Viv had never even skipped out on a nail appointment. No, she was too dependable for this type of erratic behavior.

Mary's head pounded with pain as she considered how normal Viv had been until she'd married Sam. How long had it been since she'd had a hair or nail appointment? Her sister had gone from glamour gal to tree hugger, and Mary was partly to blame.

Their current crisis with Viv began when GiGi had pushed her to go out with Sam as a hoax. He was involved with the cult that Mary and Philip had been pulled into, so Viv's job, per her mother's persuasive instruction, was to expose the cult for what it was. To save Mary. How could they have ever guessed that Viv would be dragged down too? Just as Mary and Philip were seeing the light and pulling away from the cult, Viv was marching down the aisle and giving her life to Sam. The pang of guilt made Mary shudder.

No matter how hard she tried to figure out solutions to their family's problems, nothing made sense. Finally, as had become her habit, she gave up and gave in to her truth. It was the only answer. Even though Mary initially believed she was making her way out of purgatory, she now accepted that she might actually be falling deeper into the death dream. The more she fought it, the deeper she seemed to fall. With acceptance came clarity, and with clarity came a decision. Even within her alternate reality, Mary would find her sister. And in doing so, she'd sort out the next step of her purgatory journey. There would be no more doubting it and no more fighting it. Mary was definitely dead.

*****

"Pops," GiGi said, waking him up in the middle of the night, "are you awake?" She flicked on the light from the switch above her bedside table. "Pops, wake up." She nudged him as he snored.

After a few pokes in his ribs, Poppy finally gurgled an answer. "What's wrong with you?" he asked, careful not to open his eyes. "I was finally asleep."

The sooner he could get back to sleep, the better. Sleep was his only escape from the horrible reality that had become his family's life story. Managing it had become a challenge.

"I've figured it out, sweetie, and couldn't wait until morning to tell you." GiGi's voice sounded rational enough, but she never called her husband sweetie and rarely used such a kind, thoughtful voice. Softness wasn't really the old bird's style.

"Did you just call me sweetie?" he asked, sitting up and squinting his eyes half open. His contorted face displayed complete disapproval of the whole middle-of-the-night shebang his wife was triggering.

Looking over at her husband, GiGi smiled. "Yes, sweetie, I did."

Twice. She'd called him sweetie two times in a row. Something was definitely wrong.

"What exactly did you figure out?" he asked, hoping this was not a nightmare. At any moment, it was entirely possible that his wife's head would begin spinning around as she spewed green slime from her nostrils. Poppy was only sure of two things at that moment. Number one, nothing in their lives was anywhere near normal. And number two, something about his wife's sudden onset of gentility wasn't sitting right.

"Go on and speak up," he said, prying his eyes open and giving the appearance that he was actually interested in what she had to say. "You woke me up in the middle of the night, so this better be good."

"None of this is real, Pops," she began, her eyes bright with wonder. "We are alive inside of Mary's death dream and are only semiconscious on some kind of spiritual level as she journeys toward heaven from purgatory." She spoke with confidence. "And that's why I can call you sweetie…because none of this is real." Taking a deep breath, GiGi couldn't help but to throw a barb. "In the real world, somewhere other than this, I'm sure I'm still snoring right now, dreaming of what a pain in my butt you are most of the time."

She cackled. It was an odd sort of laugh that caused Poppy's stomach to feel all strange and woozy. What was up with his wife?

"You're kidding, right?" he asked, hoping against hope that this was a big joke. "We're Baptists, and we don't even believe in purgatory."

GiGi shook her head. "No, Pops, I'm not kidding. This is as real as the tongue in my mouth." She stuck her tongue out at him playfully. "In a fantastic sort of way, I reckon, we're *purgatory peddlers*. And our job in this alternate reality is to help Mary get to heaven." She spoke as if spinning a fantastical tale. "We're living in a prayer. It makes perfect sense to me now. Mare Bear did die during childbirth when she was having Miss Charity. And I'm accepting it."

Poppy, unsure of what twilight zone he'd entered, cleared his throat and answered with trepidation. "But Mary didn't die, because we were with her that day in the hospital when our baby girl was born, and we've been by her side ever since." Caution was leading him. He felt baffled. "You're here with me now…you just woke me up from a deep sleep that I really needed…and I'm sorry to tell you, but this *is* reality."

GiGi's face beamed. "You're so darned cute, even in this death dream."

Poppy's jaw dropped open. Not only had she called him a sweetie, but now she was calling him cute. This was not good.

"In this reality, which I guess is just as real as the reality where Mary has passed into purgatory," she said, "she is very much alive. But in the real world, where we're probably helping Philip take care of Miss Charity, our daughter is gone."

His eyes, which were now wide open, nearly bugged out of his head. "Oh no," he said, taking a big swallow. It was all he could think of to say.

GiGi giggled. Her giggle turned into a belly laugh that quickly morphed into near hysteria. "Mary's been trying to tell us she's trapped inside of a death dream, and we've been fighting her every step of the way, when all along it was our job to just go along and help her find heaven. It's wonderful, ain't it, Pops? We get to be with Mary right now, even though she's pushing up daisies in the cemetery." GiGi fell back on the bed with giggles, unable to maintain any control. She appeared to be so happy with the new realization.

Poppy laid back down and pulled the covers up to his ears. If he could quickly fall back asleep, maybe all of this nonsense would be forgotten.

"And do you know the best part of all of this?" she asked, sitting straight up in the bed. "Since this is a death dream, Aggie didn't beat me in that chili cook-off after all." GiGi yanked back the covers from her husband and pulled his eyelids open with her fingers. "Who knows? Maybe outside of this death dream, Pip and Aggie are still livin' in Florida?" All was right in her world again.

Poppy, still not completely sure he wasn't in the middle of a nightmare, pinched himself. "Wake up, Pops," he said, speaking out loud to himself.

He couldn't remain silent on the issue, could he? He was surer than ever that at any given moment his wife's head would begin to spin...or maybe his own head would start turning around. Yes, GiGi was acting more lovable than she'd ever acted in her life, but what she'd suggested was far too bombastic for him to just let go.

Poppy pulled himself up to his elbows. The lines on his face settled into worry. "No, GiGi, we're not purgatory peddlers, and we're not living in Mary's death dream either," he assured her, unable to believe he'd just used the phrase 'purgatory peddlers.' But his words only served to make her giggle more.

"It's the truth, Pops," she snorted, "and as soon as you can grasp it, the happier you'll be. Just look at how happy I am."

She was happy. And friendly. He actually liked this side of his wife very much.

"Are you drunk?" he asked, jabbing one of his fingers into her ribs. Alcohol had never touched his wife's lips in all the years they'd been together, and he knew it. She wouldn't even take cough medicine for fear of getting hooked. Maybe it was pills. At this point, anything was a possibility.

She laughed harder. "No, of course I'm not drunk."

"Are you taking happy pills to help you deal with all of our problems, honey? If you are, I can get you help before you become an addict," he told her, seriously getting worried. But she started laughing so hard she had a tough time catching her breath.

"Stop talking," she hollered, still laughing, "Please, just don't say anything else. I can't take it no more. I might pee myself!"

Poppy honestly began to fret.

"You can't go losing your mind, woman, because somebody's gotta stay halfway grounded alongside me," he said as he watched her rolling around on the bed, holding her sides as she hooted and howled. GiGi was quite possibly passing over into la-la land.

"Lordy, you've completely lost it. You're gone," he said with a big groan. The man couldn't think of anything worse than losing his partner. GiGi was sometimes a hot mess, but she was the one constant in his life. He'd had lost Mary to the death dreams and Viv to her lover, and now GiGi was mentally leaving him too. Perhaps they were all in a death dream. Who was he to question anything anymore?

Silence finally fell upon the room as GiGi's giggles settled down. "You know I'm kidding around, right?" she asked. "Even though I sometimes wish I was living inside of some death dream, because reality is kicking my butt." Giving a quick half grin, she added: "I really wanted to win that darned chili cook-off, you know?"

Poppy laughed. Even though his wife was balancing family issues that would wreck most people, she was still finding levity in it all. He sighed a breath of relief. "I was hoping against hope that you were kidding," he said, feeling thankful that his wife was still sane. "But you woke me up in the middle of the night to act all crazy, for what? Are you trying to cause me to have a heart attack?"

GiGi broke out in tears. And it was an ugly cry. "I can't sleep, Pops…I'm sorry, but I just didn't feel like being up all night alone. I'm feeling scared."

Poppy pulled her close to him. "I'm not sleeping too good, either," he said. "Next time, though, instead of playing a prank on me, just ask me to stay up and keep you company. Deal?"

GiGi, tears still falling like a rain storm, patted his chest with a loud thump. "Deal," she answered.

"And for the record," he added, "your chili is the best of them all. Aggie's cooking can't hold a candle to yours. You know that, don't you?"

Grabbing a tissue from her bedside table, she blew her nose hard. "Of course I do." she said, already feeling better.

He'd known exactly what she needed to hear.

Chapter 25

Pip and Aggie had been pushed and prodded into offering support to Mary and her parents. Not only did they have a connection due to sharing duties as grandparents with GiGi and Poppy, but they also shared the same church family. As a result, if Aggie didn't show up and show out, the good Christian people in town would notice. Having a stellar reputation around town mattered more to Philip's mother than the Revlon hair dye she'd been using since her thirtieth birthday. That was saying a lot.

Preacher Walker and Jeannie had called a meeting at the old white house. They'd put Aggie in charge of bringing food, while Pip was told to be prepared to read some scripture. Viv had been AWOL for four days, while Michael had been absent for nearly two months. The family wasn't holding up too well.

It was now presumed by almost everyone in town that the two had followed through on an elaborate plan to run off together. The gossip papers jokingly referred to the tryst as "An Affair to Remember." Viv had become the exact opposite of who she'd always hoped to be. She was now the jestee, the chump, and the unfaithful adultress. Unbeknownst to her, she'd already been fired from her job as well. Viv's character was effectively ruined.

With everyone seated around the great room, Preacher Walker addressed the family. Soft spoken by nature, his folksy charm quickly put the small audience at ease. He began with prayer, asked Pip to read a few verses of scripture, and then opened the floor for the family to speak about their concerns. Aggie, meanwhile, worked feverishly in the kitchen setting up the food.

One by one, the family opened up about their concerns, thoughts, and fears. But no one addressed the giant pink elephant in the room. In fact, death dreams and sexual immorality weren't mentioned at all.

Aggie, ready to get things moving along, spoke up from the kitchen. "Preacher Walker, I thought we were here to discuss how this family is on the precipice of losing their ever-loving minds," she began, mustering all the southern hospitality she could bear on such an occasion. If she hated anything worse than being around GiGi, it was being guilted into serving the old bat. "You told Pip and me that we were coming over here to discuss Mary's death-dream debacle and Viv's vulgarity. The devil has obviously taken hold of this family, and if we're going to have a laying on of hands, let's get to it. Pip and I don't have all day, you know."

GiGi just about croaked. Who was Aggie to offer her opinion on their personal business?

At the same time Aggie was offering her spiel, she was gracefully walking toward the group, balancing a silver serving tray on the open palm of her hand. With a smile plastered upon her face, GiGi's nemesis gave a friendly nod toward the pastor when she reached them. "May I offer a pig in a blanket to anyone? They are simply scrumptious if I must say so myself."

The woman was a nightmare.

Preacher Walker rarely stumbled over his words, but after Aggie dropped the bombshell, he didn't quite know how to recover. All the eyes in the room opened wide. He'd brought Pip and Aggie over to GiGi's home to analyze their confidential secrets. The cat was out of the bag. This was an intervention.

"Oh, my dear Lord," sang GiGi, in a shrill voice, "How could you betray our confidence, Preacher Walker? Aggie has diarrhea of the mouth, and she'll tell the world about our business." GiGi grabbed her husband's hand. She was not only shocked but clearly unhappy. "This family will never live all of this down. I'm telling you, the gossip train has done left the station, and her caboose is nearly as wide as her big fat mouth."

Aggie, unable to remain quiet, was quick to defend herself. "What are you worried about? Everyone in your family is already the brunt of every joke in town. If Mary's in a death dream, what does it matter to Mary if people talk about her? It's just a dream, right Mary?"

Mary dropped her head and said nothing. She knew her former mother-in-law's attack was more about goading GiGi than it was about her.

"And as for Viv," Aggie continued, barely taking a breath, "she sent a letter and admitted to the love affair with Michael, so it must not be a big secret." Aggie snagged one of the pigs in a blanket from the tray and took a bite. "All I'm saying is that you must've done something really wrong in raising those girls to have ended up in this mess, and we've come here with Preacher Walker and Jeannie, to pray for you for the sake of the grandchildren we share."

Poppy, GiGi, and Mary had been pushed to their limit. They'd been dragged out to the playground by life and had been smacked down and beaten to a pulp. Their minds, as a result, were refusing to click on all cylinders. Paranoia had set in with fear, worry, and a lack of sleep.

As much as GiGi hated to admit it, Aggie had made a good point. Everyone in town was already aware of their personal problems; it's the downside of a small town. So what did it matter if Aggie was throwing it in their faces?

The room fell silent, and in the awkwardness of the lingering moments, Aggie placed the tray filled with pigs in a blanket on a coffee table and hustled back to the kitchen. She'd known how the family was suffering and had exploited their misery for her own selfish desire to crush an enemy from her childhood days. Guilt wasn't a feeling she was very accustomed to. She'd said too much.

Miss Charity waddled in from the next room and found Aggie in the kitchen. Grabbing her sippy cup, the little girl handed it to her other grandmother, the one who appeared to know how to get her some water really fast. Her eyes gazed upward to meet Aggie's. The innocence and frailty of the girl crashed into the shame Aggie was already feeling and caused her to break down and cry. Falling to her knees, she pulled Miss Charity into her arms and hugged her tight. "What am I doing?" she asked. "When I speak ill of Mary, GiGi, and Viv, I'm speaking about *your* family ... and you don't even have a voice to defend them."

As the two embraced, understanding washed over Aggie. Her mind opened up to the reality of the heavy burdens the family in the next room had been carrying, and her pride toppled over as it was replaced with a generous spattering of regret. No matter her feelings for GiGi, she had to give the woman credit for being such a support to her family. GiGi had even purchased the old white house so Mary and the kids could keep their home after the divorce. Now one of her children was missing, and all Aggie could do was belittle her.

Pulling Miss Charity out in front of her so they could see one another, eye to eye, she wiped away tears and whispered, "You know what? If I'd gone through all your family is going through, I probably would've run away by now." She softly giggled. "But not your GiGi. She has dug her heels into the earth and is still standing with her family. You're blessed to have her in your life, you know?" Aggie knew it was the truth. Standing to her feet, she took the little girl's hand. "Let's get you some water and then go offer some needed support to your old bird of a GiGi, what do you say?"

Nearby, Miss Charity's angel was seated up high on the kitchen countertop. God's plan was in action. The celestial guardian gave Miss Charity a playful thumbs-up, and the little girl smiled. They were a really good team.

Chapter 26

Viv and Michael, knowing they'd never be able to convince Sam to set them free, spent every waking minute trying to figure out a way to escape. The bed, welded together and bolted to the floor and walls, wasn't going anywhere. And their chains were holding strong. When they were alone in the cabin, they repeatedly hit their chains against the bed, trying to see if something might give. This went on for hours and hours until both of their wrists were bruised and sore.

Each day, they were forced to listen to either a sermon or a reading of scripture on a recorder that was in the main room. If they could've reached it, they would've smashed it to smithereens. God had been incredibly distorted in Sam's mind. He'd missed the entire person of Jesus. Love and forgiveness were replaced with what he saw as holy justice and swift judgment. Viv couldn't imagine how a group of people who are truly seeking God could fall into the clutches of a false religion, a cult....and how it could be twisted so much that murder was an acceptable choice. She'd been a part of it long enough to know they were in an impossible situation. There was no way out.

*****

After Aggie apologized to the group, the whole tenor in the white house changed. It's funny, really, how the admission of a wrong can quickly lead to finding common ground and breaking down walls. GiGi, being the spirited rube that she could be sometimes, wasn't anywhere near ready to full-on embrace Aggie. For the sake of Viv though, she was willing to put aside her grievances for a few hours. It was when the bunch adjourned to the kitchen table for a bite of lunch that things began to really shift.

Off the cuff, without any motive or thought-out agenda, GiGi asked, "Has anyone else noticed anything strange about Sam's behavior? I mean, we haven't heard from him since he left. And wouldn't you think he'd be eager to keep us updated?" She took a breath, but before anyone else could speak, she continued. "He says he's already forgiven Viv, but how is that even possible given that she's likely having all kinds of sex with another man? Pardon my frankness, but if Viv can get Michael over Sam, she's gonna boot Sam to the curb. Michael is a far better catch than that bearded cult follower."

Mary interrupted. "Mother, Rose and Ruby don't really need to hear this."

GiGi quickly rethought the tenor of her diatribe. "You're right, Mary. And I'm sorry." She grinned toward the girls, took a roll in hand, and lifted it up toward them as a sign of solace. They returned her smile with grins of their own. They'd heard it all in their short lives. Nothing she could say would shock them.

"I just don't think I'm buying Sam's crap," she said, jumping back on her soap box. "It all seems suspicious to me how Sam just took off to look for Viv, leaving these young girls behind without much of a plan at all. Who does that?"

It was one of those times when lack of sleep had likely kicked in. GiGi was talking out loud, but she was really just thinking out loud to herself, not expecting a response.

The adults at the table busily ate their food, trying not to look her way. To encourage her would've been a big mistake, and they all knew it. GiGi's words made them uncomfortable, of course, because they were worried for how Rose and Ruby might be processing the sudden change in their world. Ignoring her, they hoped, would serve to shut her up.

In a moment of silence, when GiGi finally took a bite of food, Rose, who was oblivious to rhetorical-type questions and the ramblings of the aged, responded. "I've noticed something strange about my new dad." She then popped a green bean into her mouth and chewed.

Unlike GiGi, Rose was not tired or rambling. On any other day, the adults might have ignored such a young girl. They were all so caught up in the aftermath of chaos that taking time for the jabber of a child who couldn't possibly appreciate the weightiness of all they were dealing with was an unlikely scenario. After Aggie's bona fide apology, however, hearts were warm, open, and receptive.

GiGi didn't miss a beat; her granddaughter's disclosure piped her into immediate action. "Spill the beans, sugar," she shouted, banging the table with the palm of her hand and looking straight into Rose's eyes. "Give us the dirt on your daddy."

Rose, who happened to have another green bean between her fingers, dropped it onto the table. "He looks at naked people on the computer," she whispered. "I saw him do it."

Chapter 27

The dandelion, which is not only prevalent but revered in the south for its ability to withstand the summer heat, is the only flower representing the three celestial bodies of the sun, moon, and stars. The yellow flower represents the sun, the puff ball represents the moon, and the dispersing seeds beautifully embody the stars of the sky when the wind blows them haplessly into the air. Viv and Michael, whose story had become deeply layered and complex, felt hope drifting away just like the dandelion stars. And they were unsure if they could withstand the heat.

All walls were down. Having to use a compostable toilet will do that rather quickly to a couple of lovers who are chained to the same bed. Over the hours they'd spent together, they'd shared their darkest secrets and their deepest dreams. Tales had been told, love had been made, and fears had been uncovered through both laughter and tears. The summation couldn't have been clearer. They were always meant to be together.

Sin, though, was the word on their tongues that day. Viv was married, and having a love affair with Michael, no matter how right it felt, could never be right in the sight of God. As humans do, they were guilty of trying to take the edge off of their actions. Viv was married to an abuser, after all, and wouldn't

God make an exception for that? All debating aside on the issue, they knew the truth. Outside of the bounds of marriage, sex is sin. All sin comes with a price, so God wouldn't be saving them.

The more Viv and Michael discussed God's truth, the more they began to accept their sin as equal to the sin of Michael and Bonnie. The act of sin, after all, is an unrelenting measure of one's heart. Whether one steals, kills, or covets doesn't really matter. Pride, the base rejection of the Sculptor who created the human race and the Author who is writing the on-going story, is at the root of all evil. Life is black and white. There is no sin that's better than another.

Salvation, then, is necessarily equal to full and complete submission. It's the intentional handing over of one's life to a holy and just God. It's realizing humankind's place in the world. And the surrender must happen at every cognitive moment. Because once a human being takes his life into his own hands, he's no longer held safe under the mighty pinions of God. Just as Adam and Eve felt themselves to be naked and unprotected in the Garden of Eden, Viv and Michael now realized their spiritual nakedness.

"We deserve what's coming to us," Viv lamented, holding Michael's hands in her own. "We deserve death." As the truth settled in, she felt angry and terrified. "We could just take our own lives. Why prolong death when it's coming for us anyway? And why give Sam and Bonnie the pleasure of slitting our throats?"

Michael released one of his hands to wipe a tear from his cheek. "We do deserve death, Viv, but we serve a mighty redeemer who loves us in spite of our sin."

Truth spilled from her lover's heart, and God's power sprang forth from his tongue. Michael couldn't have held it back if he'd wanted to. The truth had set him free. "He's our Father, and we will never be beyond His reach, no matter how much we sin. His word says nothing can separate us from His love… and even now, in this cabin out in the middle of nowhere, He is as close as our shadow."

A momentary smile slipped from Michael's face as he considered the love of God, so grand and awesome, but just as quickly, his smile was replaced with concern. Mentally, Viv was breaking down. He couldn't believe she'd mentioned suicide.

"You'd never really consider killing yourself, would you?" he asked, worry causing the faint lines on his face to become more visible. "Viv, please tell me you'd never hurt yourself."

Overcome with exhaustion, Viv began to weep. Her shoulders shook as she cried. The tears poured from her eyes as she considered the tiny speck of history she occupied.

She'd been so angry with God when the abuse began with Sam. Hadn't she waited years for the right man to come along? And when she finally settled down with a man who proclaimed to love the Lord with all his heart, she quickly learned she'd been duped. She'd saved herself for nothing. He was a beast.

And oh how she'd resented Rose and Ruby. They represented her failure to get pregnant and all the many times she'd been hit because of it. She knew her daughters had come from a traumatic past, but had she shown them mercy and patience? No, not at all. She'd been harsh with them. She'd complained about them. Sometimes she'd even despised them.

And in her darkest hour of all, she'd knowingly and purposefully turned to sexual sin with Michael. Even now, if he asked, she'd spit in God's face and have sex with the man she loved. Viv longed to feel beautiful and wanted to be held with kind hands and spoken to with passionate words. Michael did all of that and more. He was now her god. Her savior.

No, Viv wasn't holy. Far from it.

There were times during her marriage with Sam when she'd stopped believing in God. But now, she'd come to accept His very real existence. She hated Him. And He hated her. How had her life spun so out of control?

Viv had been brought up in church. She'd read the Bible, had given her heart to Christ, and had been baptized as a child. She'd surrendered her will to Him. The thought caused rage to rise up in her. Tears continued to flow from her face. Why had she ever believed that God gives good gifts to His children? Isn't that what Preacher Walker had preached? It was a lie.

Michael, trying to comfort the woman he now loved more than he could ever imagine loving another person, continued speaking as she cried. "We've prayed, baby. We've admitted our sin and have asked God to forgive us. His word says if we confess our sins, He is faithful and just to forgive us and to cleanse us from all unrighteousness. Do you believe God is a liar?"

Viv shook her head. "Of course not," she answered, not wanting Michael to see the true depth of her depravity. "I'm tired, and I just don't feel worthy of forgiveness...I guess I sometimes believe I deserve to be punished." She wasn't about to reveal the workings of her mind to Michael. If she did, she might lose him. She'd let him go on believing in the goodness of the kind carpenter who became a Savior if it brought him happiness. And whatever Michael asked her to agree to, she would agree. He was her sole purpose for living.

Michael pulled Viv's chin up with his hands. He was so gentle with her. Keeping her chin pinched between his fingers, he spoke with such calm reassurance. "Everyone who has ever taken a breath in the history of the world has sinned, Viv. And we all deserve death. That's why the Savior came and took it all upon Himself. We needed Him because we couldn't do it on our own."

From the time she could crawl, Viv had been taught about Jesus and how He'd sacrificed everything for her. All Michael's words were words she'd heard and believed her entire life. Now, however, the words had lost their driving force. She'd become the woman in a long skirt who wore a doily on her head as a head covering. She'd followed all sorts of rules for God. She'd remained married to an abuser for God. She'd adopted two hooligan children for God. And where had it gotten her?

"Right now, let's calm down and agree to put our sin behind us," he said. "The Bible says God has removed our sins from us…as far as the East is from the West…so let's accept His forgiveness, forgive ourselves, and move forward. Your sister's life may depend on us."

At the mere mention of Mary, Viv snapped out of the haze of despair and pulled all the dandelion stars right back into her grasp. She had to keep it together for her sister. If Sam and Bonnie followed through on their plan, Mary would be their next victim.

Wiping her tears away, she leaned forward and wrapped her arms around Michael's neck. Resolute and strong, she spoke frankly. "I'm all right now. I think I just needed an emotional girl cry." She feigned laughter with a slight giggle and hint of embarrassment. "I'm such a girl."

All the tension left Michael as he felt relief from her hug. "Well, I think under the circumstances, you're allowed to have an emotional girl cry," he said, hugging her tight. "And for the record, I love that you're such a girl." He loved her and wanted to believe she was truly OK.

Pulling back, Viv placed her hands firmly on his shoulders. "Michael, promise me you won't let Bonnie and Sam hurt Mary, OK? Promise me you'll find an answer."

"I promise," he answered, taking his pointer finger and dotting the end of her nose.

Filled with gratitude and trust, Viv reached her arms back round his neck and embraced him as tightly as her body would allow. He then bowed his head and closed his eyes. "Lord, send us help. Please, we need your help and we need you to spare Mary from this horror. We trust You…and we thank you in advance for all you're going to do on our behalf. Amen."

As he prayed, Viv wondered what Michael would do once she was gone. She couldn't live with the pain. Suicide seemed like the best answer. God wasn't going to send help. God hated her. And she hated Him.

Chapter 28

When Sam saw GiGi's number come across the screen on his cell phone, he answered. She asked him to meet her at the restaurant where Viv had planned to meet a client on the night of her mysterious disappearance. He agreed.

The old bird planned to light into him with both barrels loaded after hearing about his porno problem from Rose. To say she was shocked would've been an understatement. Sam, after all, was in a cult. He practically stuffed the King James version of the Bible down her throat every time she brought up a new country hit song or a rated-R movie. Something was very wrong. She would peck his eyes out before she'd let him look at another naked woman on a computer screen in the presence of her grandchildren.

Sam was waiting at a small round table when she arrived. He'd already ordered a couple of sweet iced teas and stood to greet his mother-in-law with a customary hug. She waved him off with her hand, pulled out her chair, and plopped down. The woman was not happy, that much was evident.

"Obviously, something's on your mind," he said, sitting back down and placing a napkin across his lap. GiGi just stared at him. She couldn't get over how different he looked without the straggly beard and unkempt hair.

"Is that sculpting gel in your hair, Sam?" she asked, noting how neat his hair looked. "And where on earth is your bushy beard? Please tell me you've finally left the cult."

He *was* wearing gel. Sam looked very much like a changed man. "I'm fightin' psoriasis," he mumbled, taking his glass of iced tea in his hand and swirling it around. "That's why I shaved my beard and cut my hair. What's the big deal?"

The big deal, obviously, was that his beard and long hair were tied inextricably to his religious beliefs. She'd attended the cult a few times and knew the expectations the group put upon their followers.

"Really, Sam?" she asked, her eyebrows raised and a goofy grin across her face. "Do I look like I've been hit with a stupid stick? You ain't got the psoriasis anymore than I've got the VD! I don't see ne'er a pimple on your face." She was baiting the man who'd married her daughter. GiGi had come looking for a fight.

Sam laughed out loud. GiGi had pegged him. She always did.

"Why did you want to meet me?" he asked, changing the subject. "You've obviously got some sort of bee in your bonnet today, so just say whatever you've got to say."

Sam's attitude told GiGi all she needed to know. A broken man filled with concern for his missing wife wasn't sitting before her. This was a man who was eager to spar with his mother-in-law. There was definitely a different side to Sam. She'd always suspected it, but sitting across from him in that restaurant, the final place she'd known her daughter to have been, she saw right through him.

"You want to know why I wanted to meet you?" she asked, "I'll tell you why." Placing her elbows up on the table, she leaned forward toward Sam. "To begin with, I think you're full of baloney."

*****

It was late in the evening when Viv and Michael heard Sam's car pulling up to the cabin. Bonnie had already settled in for the evening and had been tromping around braless in a white t-shirt and hot pink panties. Her blond, tousled hair was pulled up into a messy bun, but her makeup was still perfectly in place. The prisoners knew sex was on her agenda, which meant Sam would be in a good mood. This bought them at least another day.

Their routine was pretty well set. Bonnie was typically the first one to make it to the cabin in the late afternoon or early evening. She brought dinner to them and then retired to her room to watch DVDs on an old television set. Later, Sam would join her. Viv and Michael rarely saw Sam, but Bonnie was always in and out of their room, trying to stir up an argument. Power and control fed the blond bombshell, so they refused to engage.

The two were lying on the bed, trying to relax, when the front door opened.

"Where in the Sam Hill are we?"

The voice was unmistakable.

It was GiGi.

Everything from that point on happened fast. GiGi was shoved into the room with Viv and Michael and chained to the same bed. It didn't take long for the pieces of the puzzle to come together in the woman's mind. Viv hadn't run away with Michael but had been taken prisoner by Sam.

"Momma!" Viv shouted, shocked to see the one who'd given her birth. "Did Sam hurt you?"

GiGi, still trying to maintain an element of control, shook her head at Viv and continued speaking to her captor. "I sure am glad Pops insisted on having one of them trackers injected underneath my skin," she said, gritting her teeth and speaking with authority. "I was against it at first, you know, because of the mark of the beast and all, but right about now that tracker is serving its purpose. Yessir, my husband is a smart man. He'll be finding me within the next few hours."

A tracker? What was her mom babbling about? Viv couldn't believe her eyes or ears. Michael had prayed for God to send help, and God had sent GiGi. Her mother was going to be the source of their rescue.

GiGi's insides were in knots, but she showed no fear. She wanted to melt down and to grab hold of Viv's neck and to hug her tight. She wanted to say that she was sorry for judging her, to ask her if the cult man had hurt her, and to protect her above all else. She knew, however, that showing weakness would only serve to put all their lives in further jeopardy.

"That's right," she chirped, "my tracker is being put to work right now. And it's hidden in a place you'd never suspect." Patting her body haphazardly, seemingly to throw Sam off, she continued. "That tracker is somewhere on this body, deep underneath my skin, but you'd never find it even if you tried."

Sam chuckled. "Don't worry, I ain't gonna go huntin' around for a tracker on your body, GiGi."

In response to the big scene, Bonnie, equally as shocked as Viv, grabbed Sam and pulled him into the main room. "What the hell is *she* doing here? This was not our plan."

Sam, pleased with himself, explained to his lover how GiGi was a much better choice than Mary. "Just think about it," he said. "This will drive Mary even further over the edge. Once she finds out her mother is missing, she'll live forever in her imaginary death dream. It will be living torture for her, which is so much better than if we killed her off."

Bonnie hesitated. "The buzzard says she has a tracker implant, didn't you hear her? She's going to lead her husband, and probably the police, right to us."

Sam laughed. He knew GiGi was bluffing. At least he was pretty sure she was bluffing.

*****

With Bonnie and Sam out of the room, GiGi had time to speak. "Are you two OK?" she asked, checking out the chain that currently bound her to the bed. Concern was written plainly all over her face.

Both Viv and Michael nodded their heads in unison. They were happy to see a familiar face. Michael quickly explained that they'd be better off to remain quiet but assured her that they'd fill her in on all the details once Sam and Bonnie were asleep. GiGi heeded the advice and looked forward to dissecting the madness.

Viv, however, still stunned by the sudden appearance of her mother, couldn't remain quiet. "I didn't know that Daddy had you injected with a tracker," she whispered, excited about the possibility of freedom. "We'll finally be saved because *my* daddy is brilliant."

GiGi just looked at her, all bug-eyed. Her daughter was too gullible. Foolish even. What had happened to the spunky girl she'd raised?

Viv noted her mother's sideways glance. "Daddy did have you injected with a tracker, right, Momma?" she asked, grabbing Michael's hand with full anticipation of being released from the makeshift prison.

GiGi shook her head. "That would be a hell to the big fat no," she whispered, balking at her daughter's stupidity. "Don't you have a sliver of common sense?" she asked, still whispering but getting louder as her annoyance began to grow. "Believe me, I would've told you if I'd ever had a tracker implanted in my body, but what that crazy cult fool don't know won't hurt him."

Viv's draw dropped open. "You lied?"

"Yes dingbat, your mother told a little white lie to a kidnapper, which I think cancels out my sin," GiGi answered, ready to punch a hole in the wall. "So either crucify me or get with the program. We need to keep *Sam The Damn Sham* off kilter if we can." The woman might've been a grandma, but she was not going down easy.

Viv couldn't believe it. As soon as hope had come, it had gone. "We're going to die," she said softly, as realization settled in. "And momma, you're going to die because of me."

GIGI knew it was probably the truth. They were all going to die at the hands of a man who honestly believed God would not only condone murder, but would be pleased with it. Without the slightest hint of self-awareness, Sam had been sucked into a false faith that focused so much on God's laws and justice, that it had forgotten all about His love, grace, and mercy. To meet him, no one would ever guess his propensity for something so gruesome as murder.

Fluffing the hair around her face, because even in the direst of circumstances, she wanted to look her best, Viv's mom cleared her throat. The words she was preparing to speak needed to be loud and clear for everyone in the cabin, including Sam, to hear. "Come hell or high water, I will not die at the hand of a yellow-bellied coward, Viv, and neither will you!"

If she'd taught her daughters anything over the years, it was that women are not the weaker sex. Viv had gotten involved with a man who enjoyed lording over her with his brute strength. He'd used her faith in God to manipulate her and had employed his physical brawn to beat her down. Sam had snuffed out the fire that had once burned inside of Viv, and GiGi hated him for it.

"How are Rose and Ruby?" Viv asked, searching for a smile but only finding half of one. She'd always admired her mother's strength, but never as much as she did in that moment.

GiGi grabbed her daughter's knee and squeezed it hard. "They're strong, because they've had to be strong. I really believe there is solid potential in those girls." Her voice cracked with emotion, and she paused for a couple of seconds as she thought of how attached she'd already become to her new granddaughters. "But they need their momma and their GiGi to be there for them and to teach them how to not be taken in by the Sam Smiths of the world. We've got to get back to them, OK?" She winked her eye, shot her daughter a sly grin, and exuded an air of confidence that she didn't feel.

Tied to a bed in a small cabin in the middle of the woods, GiGi made a secret vow to herself. She would reignite the burning fire of strength and confidence inside of Viv. Though they may die, they'd die fighting. And so even in death, if it came to that, they'd make their family proud.

www.ingramcontent.com/pod-product-compliance
Lightning Source LLC
Chambersburg PA
CBHW070850120626
46556CB00002B/945